# The Larkville Legacy

*A secret letter...two families changed forever.*

Welcome to the small town of Larkville, Texas, where
the Calhoun family has been ranching
for generations.

Meanwhile, in New York, the Patterson family rules
America's highest echelons of society.

Both families are totally unprepared for the news that
they are linked by a shocking secret. For hidden on the
Calhoun ranch is a letter that's been lying unopened
and unread—until now!

Meet the two families in all 8 books
of this brand-new series:

*The Cowboy Comes Home* by Patricia Thayer

*Slow Dance with the Sheriff* by Nikki Logan

*Taming the Brooding Cattleman* by Marion Lennox

*The Rancher's Unexpected Family* by Myrna Mackenzie

*His Larkville Cinderella* by Melissa McClone

*The Secret That Changed Everything* by Lucy Gordon

*The Soldier's Sweetheart* by Soraya Lane

*The Billionaire's Baby SOS* by Susan Meier

Dear Reader,

Writing a book as part of a series about a whole family is particularly fascinating because we come to know so much of the heroine's background.

As we grow up, the influences that shape us are so many and so varied that it's hard to see the real person without knowing about them. Much of Charlotte's life has been one thing while seeming to be another. She comes from a happy, loving family with two parents, two sisters and a brother. What could be better?

But she's tormented by the feeling of being the odd one out, less attractive and talented than the others, and her adventurous spirit has sometimes led her to act rebelliously. Seeking escape, she takes off for a year in Italy. But in Rome, she learns of a shattering family secret, and finds that she's the last to know.

Devastated, she falls into the arms of Lucio, a fiercely attractive Italian. But their night together results in a baby. Lucio is glad—but is it *her* that he wants or only the child? And how much is he driven by a past even more troubled than her own? Surely loving him is too great a risk? Won't she, once again, be the odd one out?

Perhaps she will never know his true feelings for her. Or perhaps a family reunion will unexpectedly give her the answer she can only dream of.

With best wishes,

Lucy Gordon

# LUCY GORDON

## The Secret That Changed Everything

HARLEQUIN®
entertain, enrich, inspire™

Recycling programs
for this product may
not exist in your area.

ISBN-13: 978-0-373-17848-3

THE SECRET THAT CHANGED EVERYTHING

First North American Publication 2012

Copyright © 2012 by Harlequin Books S.A.

Special thanks and acknowledgment are given to Lucy Gordon
for her contribution to The Larkville Legacy series.

**Lucy Gordon** cut her writing teeth on magazine journalism, interviewing many of the world's most interesting men, including Warren Beatty, Charlton Heston and Roger Moore. She also camped out with lions in Africa, and had many other unusual experiences which have often provided the background for her books. Several years ago, while staying in Venice, she met a Venetian who proposed to her after two days. They have been married ever since. Naturally this has affected her writing, where romantic Italian men tend to feature strongly.

Two of her books have won a Romance Writers of America RITA® Award.

You can visit her website, www.lucy-gordon.com.

**Books by Lucy Gordon**

PLAIN JANE IN THE SPOTLIGHT
MISS PRIM AND THE BILLIONAIRE
RESCUED BY THE BROODING TYCOON
HIS DIAMOND BRIDE
A MISTLETOE PROPOSAL

**Other titles by this author available in ebook format.**

# PROLOGUE

He was there!

After such an anxious search it was hard to be sure at first; aged about thirty, tall, lean, fit, with black hair. Was it really him? But then he made a quick movement and Charlotte knew.

This was the man she'd come to find.

He'd looked different last time, elegantly dressed, smooth, sophisticated, perfectly at home in one of the most fashionable bars in Rome. Now, in the Tuscan countryside, he was equally at home in jeans and casual shirt, absorbed in the vines that streamed in long lines under the setting sun. So absorbed that he didn't look up to see her watching him from a distance.

Lucio Constello.

Quickly she pulled out a scrap of paper and checked his name. At the back of her mind a wry voice murmured that if you'd sought out a man to tell him devastating news it was useful to get his name right. On the other hand, if you'd only exchanged first names, and he'd left while you were still asleep, who could he blame but himself?

She tried to silence that voice. It spoke to her too often these days.

She began to walk the long path between the vines, trying to calm her thoughts. But they refused to be calmed. They lingered rebelliously on the memory of his naked body against hers, the heat of his breath, the way he'd murmured her name.

There had been almost a question in his voice, as though he was asking her if she were certain. But there was no certainty left in her life. Her family, her boyfriend—these were the things she had clung to. But her boyfriend had rejected her and the foundations of her family had been shaken. So she'd invited Lucio to her bed because—what did it matter? What did anything matter?

He was looking up, suddenly very still as he saw her. What did that stillness mean? That he recognised her and guessed why she was here? Or that he'd forgotten a woman he'd known for a few hours several weeks ago?

When Lucio first looked up the sun was in his eyes, blinding him, so that for a moment he could make out no details. A woman was approaching him down the long avenue of vines, her attention fixed on him as though only he mattered in all the world.

That had happened so many times before. So often he'd seen Maria coming towards him from a great distance.

But Maria was dead.

The woman approaching him now was a stranger and yet mysteriously familiar. Her eyes were fixed on him even at a distance.

And he knew that nothing in the world was ever going to be the same again.

# CHAPTER ONE

GOING to Italy had seemed a brilliant move for a language expert. She could improve her Italian, study the country and generally avoid recognising that she wasn't just leaving New York; she was fleeing it.

But the truth was still the truth. Charlotte knew she had to flee memories of an emotion that had once felt like love, but which had revealed itself as disappointingly hollow, casting a negative light on almost everything in her life. It was like wandering in a desert. She belonged to nobody and nobody belonged to her. Perhaps it was this thought that made her leave her laptop computer behind. It pleased her to be beyond the reach of anyone unless she herself decided otherwise.

For two months she wandered around Italy, seeking something she couldn't define. She made a point of visiting Naples, fascinated by the legendary Mount Vesuvius, whose eruptions had destroyed cities in the past. Disappointingly it was now considered so safe that she could wander up to the summit and stand there listening hopefully for a growl.

Silence.

Which was a bit like her life, she thought wryly. Waiting for something significant to happen. But nothing did. At twenty-seven, an age when many people had chosen their path in life, she still had no clue where hers was leading.

On the train from Naples to Rome she thought of Don, the man she'd briefly thought she loved. She'd wanted commitment and when Don didn't offer it she'd demanded to know where they were headed. His helpless shrug had told her the worst, and she'd hastened to put distance between them.

She had no regrets. Briefly she'd wondered if she might have been cleverer and perhaps drawn him closer instead of driving him away. But in her heart she knew things had never been quite right between them. It was time to move on.

But where?

As the train pulled into Roma Termini she reckoned it might be interesting to find the answer to that question.

She took a taxi to the Hotel Geranno on the Via Vittorio Veneto, one of the most elegant and expensive streets in Rome. The hotel boasted every facility, including its own internet café. She found it easily and slipped into a booth, full of plans to contact family and friends. She might even get in touch with Don on her social networking site, just to let him know there were no hard feelings, and they could be friends.

But the words that greeted her on Don's page were 'Thanks to everyone for your kind wishes on my engagement. Jenny and I want our wedding to be—'

She shut the file down.

Jenny! Charlotte remembered her always hanging around making eyes at Don. And he'd noticed her. Pretty, sexy, slightly voluptuous—she was made to be noticed.

*Not like me,* she thought.

Some women would have envied Charlotte's appearance. Tall, slender, dark-haired, dark-eyed; she wasn't a woman who faded into the background. She'd always had her share of male admiration; not the kind of gawping leer that Jenny could inspire, but satisfying enough. Or so she'd thought.

But Don hadn't wasted any time mourning her and that was just fine. The past was the past.

She touched a few more keys to access her email, and immediately saw one from her sister Alex, headlined, You'll never believe this!

Alex liked to make things sound exciting so, although mildly intrigued, Charlotte wasn't alarmed. But, reading the email, she grew still again as a family catastrophe unfolded before her eyes.

'Mom—' she murmured. 'You couldn't have—*it's not possible!*'

She had always known that her father, Cedric Patterson, was her mother's second husband. Before him Fenella had been married to Clay Calhoun, a Texas rancher. Only after their divorce had she married Cedric and lived with him in New York. There she'd borne four children—the twins Matt and Ellie, Charlotte and her younger sister Alexandra.

Now it seems that Mom was already carrying Matt and Ellie when she left Clay, Alex wrote. She wrote and told him she was pregnant, but by that time he was with Sandra, who seems to have hidden the letter but, oddly enough, kept it. Nobody knew about it until both she and Clay were dead. He died last year, and the letter was found unopened, so I guess he never knew about Matt and Ellie.

What do you think of that? All these years we've thought they were our brother and sister, but now it seems we're only half-siblings! Same mother, different father. When Ellie told me what had happened I couldn't get my head around it, and I'm still in a spin.

Quickly Charlotte ran through her other emails, seeking one from Ellie that she was sure would be there. But she found nothing. Disbelieving, she ran through them again, but there was no word from Ellie.

Which meant that everyone in the family knew except her. Ellie hadn't bothered to tell her something so momentous. It had been left to Alex to send her the news as an afterthought, as though she was no more than a fringe member of the family. Which, right now, was how she felt.

Returning to the lobby she again knew the sensation of being lost in a desert. But this desert had doors, one leading to a restaurant known for its haute cuisine, the other leading to a bar. Right this minute a drink was what she needed.

The barman smiled as she approached. 'What can I get you?'

'A tequila,' she told him.

When it was served she looked around for a place to sit, but could see only one seat free, at the far end of the bar. She slipped into it and found that she could lean back comfortably against the wall, surveying her surroundings.

The room was divided into alcoves, some small, some large. The small ones were all taken up by couples, gazing at each other, revelling in the illusion of privacy. The larger ones were crowded with 'beautiful people' as though the cream of Roman society had gathered here tonight.

In the nearest alcove six people focused their attention on one man. He was king of all he surveyed, Charlotte thought with a touch of amusement. And with reason. In his early thirties, handsome, lean, athletic, he held centre-stage without effort. When he laughed, they laughed. When he spoke they listened.

Nice if you can get it, Charlotte thought with a little sigh. *I'll bet his volcano never falls silent.*

Just then he glanced up and saw her watching him. For the briefest moment he turned his head to one side, a question in his eyes. Then one of the women claimed his attention and he turned to her with a perfectly calculated smile.

An expert, she thought. He knows exactly what he's doing to them, and what they can do for him.

Such certainly seemed enviable. Her own future looked depressing. Returning to New York smacked of defeat. She could stay in Italy for the year she'd promised herself, but that was less inviting now that things were happening at home; things from which she was excluded.

She thought of Don and Jenny, revelling in their love. All around her she saw people happy in each other's company, smiling, reaching out. And suddenly it seemed unbearable that there was nobody reaching out to her. She finished her drink and sat staring at the empty glass.

'Excuse me, can I just—?'

It was the man from the alcove, easing himself into the slight space between her and the next bar stool. She leaned back to make space for him but a slight unevenness in the floor made him wobble and slew to the side, colliding with her.

*'Mi dispiace,'* he apologised in Italian, steadying her with his hand.

*'Va tutto bene,'* she reassured him. *'Niente di male.'* All is well. No harm done.

Still in Italian he said, 'But you'll let me buy you a drink to say sorry.'

'Thank you.'

'Another tequila?' asked the barman.

'Certainly not,' said the newcomer. 'Serve this lady a glass of the very best Chianti, then bring another round of drinks to me and my friends over there.'

He retreated and the barman placed a glass of red wine in front of Charlotte. It was the most delicious she had ever tasted. Sipping it she glanced over at him, and it was no surprise to find him watching her. She raised her glass in salute and he raised his back. This seemed to disconcert the women sitting on either side of him, who asserted themselves to reclaim him, Charlotte was amused to notice.

Despite being in the heart of Rome they were speaking English. She was sitting close enough to overhear some of the remarks passing back and forth, half sentences, words that floated into the distance, but all telling the tale of people who lived expensive lives.

'You were on that cruise, weren't you? Wasn't it a gorgeous ship? Everything you wanted on demand...'

'I knew I'd met you before...you were at the opening of that new...'

'Look at her. If she's not wearing the latest fashion she thinks...'

Leaning back, Charlotte observed the little gathering with eyes that saw everything. Two of the women were watching Lucio like lions studying prey, but they were in alliance. She could have sworn that one murmured to the other, 'Me first'. She couldn't hear the words, but she could read their expressions: watchful, confident that each would have their turn with him.

She could understand their desires. It wasn't merely his striking looks and costly clothes, but his air of being in charge, directing his own life and that of others. This was a man who'd never known doubt or fear.

She envied him. It must be good to know so certainly who you were, what you were, how others saw you and where you belonged in the world, instead of being that saddest of creatures—a woman who drank alone.

As if to emphasise the point the seat beside her was occupied by a woman gazing devotedly at her male companion, who returned the compliment with interest, then slid an arm about her shoulders, drew her close and said fervently, 'Let's go now.'

'Yes, let's,' she breathed. And they were gone.

At once the man in the alcove rose, excused himself to his companions and swiftly claimed the empty seat before anyone else could try.

'Can I get you another drink?' he asked Charlotte.

'Well, just a small one. I should be leaving.'

'Going somewhere special?'

'No,' she said softly. 'Nowhere special.'

After a moment he said, 'Are you alone?'

'Yes.'

He grinned. 'Perhaps you'd be better off with someone to protect you from clumsy guys like me.'

'No need. I can protect myself.'

'I see. No man necessary, eh?'

'Absolutely.'

A voice called, 'Hey, Lucio! Let's get going!'

His companions in the alcove were preparing to leave, beckoning him towards the door.

'Afraid I can't,' he said. 'I'm meeting someone here in half an hour. It was nice to meet you.'

Reluctantly they bid him goodbye and drifted away. When the door was safely closed he breathed out in obvious relief.

'Hey, your friends are crazy about you,' she reproved him lightly. 'You might at least return the compliment.'

'They're not my friends. I only know them casually, and two I never met before today.'

'But you were dousing them with charm.'

'Of course. I'm planning to make money out of them.'

'Ah! Hence the charm!'

'What else is charm for?'

'So now you're girding up for your next "victim" in half an hour.'

He gave a slow smile. 'There's no one coming. That was just to get rid of them.'

She looked down into her glass, lest her face reveal how much this pleased her. He would be a welcome companion for a little while.

He read her exactly, offering his hand and saying, 'Lucio—'

His last name was drowned by a merry shout from further along the bar. She raised her voice to say, 'Charlotte.'

'*Buona sera,* Charlotte.'

'*Buona sera,* Lucio.'

'Are you really Italian?' he asked, his head slightly to one side.

'Why do you ask?'

'Because I can't quite pinpoint your accent. Venice? No, I don't think so. Milan? Hmm. Rome—Naples?'

'Sicily?' Charlotte teased.

'No, not Sicily. You sound nothing like.'

'You said that very quickly. You must know Sicily well.'

'Fairly well. But we were talking about you. Where do you come from?'

His bright smile was like a visor behind which he'd retreated at the mention of Sicily. Though intrigued, she was too wise to pursue the matter just yet. Later would be more interesting.

'I'm not Italian at all,' she said. 'I'm American.'

'You're kidding me!'

'No, I'm not. I come from New York.'

'And you speak my language like a native. I'm impressed.' Someone squeezed by them, forcing them to draw back uncomfortably. 'There's no room for us here,' he said, taking her arm and drawing her towards the door.

Several pairs of female eyes regarded her with frank envy. It was clear that the watching women had their own ideas about how the evening would end.

*Well, you're wrong,* Charlotte thought, slightly irritated. *He's a nice guy and I'll enjoy talking to him, but that's all. Not everything has to end in* amore, *even in Italy. OK, so he's suave, sophisticated, expensively dressed and fantastically good-looking, but I won't hold that against him.*

'So why Italian?' he asked as they began to stroll along the Via Vittorio Veneto.

'I was always fascinated by foreign languages. I studied several at school, but somehow it was always Italian that stood out and attracted me more than the others. So I learned it through and through. It's such a lovely language.'

'And in the end you got a job here, probably working at the U.S. Embassy, just up the street.'

'No, I don't work here. I'm a translator in New York. I do Italian editions of books, sometimes universities hire me to look over old manuscripts. And I suddenly thought, it's about time I actually saw the country and drank in what it's really like. So I caught the next plane out.'

'Literally?'

'Well, it took a couple of days to make arrangements, but that's all. Then I was free to go.'

'No ties? Family?'

'I've got parents, siblings, but nobody who can constrain my freedom.'

'Freedom,' he mused. 'That's what it's really about, huh?'

'One of the things. I've done some mad, stupid things in my life, and most of them have been about staying free.' She gave a wry laugh. 'It's practically my family nickname. Ellie's the beautiful one, Alex is the lovable one and I'm the crazy one.'

'That sounds fascinating. I'd really like to hear about your craziness.'

'Well, there's the time I set my heart on marrying this guy and my parents said no. We were only seventeen, which they thought was too young.'

He considered this with an air of seriousness that had a touch of humour. 'They could have had a point.'

'The way I saw it they were denying me my own way. Hell would freeze over before I admitted they could be right. So we eloped.'

'You married at seventeen?'

'No way. By the time we'd covered a few miles I could see what a juvenile twerp he was. To be fair I think he'd spotted the same about me. Anyway, I got all set to make a run for it, and bumped into him because *he* was making a run for it, too.'

Lucio roared with laughter. 'What happened when you got home?'

'My mother's a very clever woman. She knew better than to make a fuss. When she caught me sidling in she glanced up and said, "Oh, there you are. Don't make a noise, your father's asleep." We had a talk later but there were no hysterics. By then she was used to me doing stupid things.'

'But would getting married be the path to freedom? Husbands can be very restrictive.'

She chuckled. 'I didn't think of that at the time. I just pictured him doing things my way. Luckily I saw the truth before too late.'

'Yes, husbands have this maddening habit of wanting their own way.'

'Oh, I learnt the lesson.'

'So you still don't have a husband?'

'No husband, no nothing.' She added casually, 'These days it's the way to be.'

'You're a true woman of your age. At one time an unmarried girl would wonder why no man wanted her. Now she wonders what's the best way to keep them off.'

'Right,' she responded in the same teasing voice. 'Sometimes you have to be really ingenious. And sometimes just ruthless.'

'You talk like an expert. Or like a woman who's been kicked in the teeth and is going to do some kicking back.' He saw her wry face and said quickly, 'I'm sorry, I had no right to say that. None of my business.'

'It's all right. If we all minded our own business there'd be precious little of interest to talk about.'

'I've got a feeling I should be nervous about what you're going to say next.'

'I could ask about Sicily, couldn't I? Is that where you keep a secret wife, or perhaps two secret wives? Now that would really be interesting.'

'Sorry to disappoint you but there's no wife, secret or otherwise. I was born in Sicily, but I left it years ago, and I've never been back. The life just didn't suit me. Like you, I went exploring the world, and I ended up with a family who owned vineyards. Vines, wine-making, I loved it from the start. They were wonderful to me, practically adopted me, and finally left the vineyards to me.'

And he'd turned them into a top money-making business, she thought. That was clear from the way he dressed and the way others reacted to him.

They were reaching the end of the street. As they turned the corner Charlotte stopped, astonished and thrilled by the sight that met her eyes.

'The Trevi Fountain,' she breathed. 'I've always wanted to see it. It's so huge, so magnificent....'

This was no mere fountain. A highly decorated palace wall rose behind it, at the centre of which was a triumphal arch, framing the magnificent, half-naked figure of Oceanus, mythical god of water, ruling over the showers that cascaded into the pool below. Everywhere was flooded with light, giving the water a dazzling glitter against the night.

'I've read about it,' she murmured, 'and seen pictures, but—'

'But nothing prepares you,' he agreed. 'Some things have to be experienced before they become real.'

Nearby was a café with tables out on the street. Here they could sit and watch the humming life about them.

'Nice to see people having a good time,' she murmured.

'Does that mean your life is unhappy now?'

'Oh, no,' she said quickly. 'But it does tend to be a bit too serious. Legal documents, history books. Not exactly filled with fun. And sometimes you need to remind yourself about fun.'

He regarded her curiously, thinking that a woman with her looks could have all the fun she wanted with all the men she wanted. So there was a mystery here. But he was too astute to voice the thought.

'But Italy should remind you of fun,' he said. 'It's not all cathedrals and sober history.'

'I know. You've only got to stroll the streets of Rome in the twilight, and see—well, lots of things.'

His grin and the way he nodded spoke volumes about his own life. Doubtless it was full of 'twilight activities', she thought. And they would be fun. She didn't doubt that either.

'Anyway,' she went on, 'my favourite Italian was—'

She named a historical character with a legendary reputation for wickedness.

'He wasn't as bad as people think,' Lucio observed. 'He was actually quite a serious man who—'

'Don't say that,' she interrupted him quickly. 'You'll spoil him for me. If he's not wicked he's not interesting.'

He regarded her curiously. 'There aren't many people who'd see it that way.'

'But it's true.'

'Certainly it's true, but we're not supposed to say so.'

'Well, I'm always doing things I'm not supposed to. That's why I'm the black sheep of the family.'

'Because you eloped at seventeen?'

She chuckled. 'There were a few more things than that. There was the politician who came to hold a meeting in New York, all virtue and pomposity, except that he'd spent the previous night in a place where he shouldn't have been. I'd seen him leaving and I couldn't resist getting up at the meeting and asking him about it.'

'Shame on you!' he said theatrically.

'Yes, I have no sense of propriety, so I'm told.'

'So you're wicked and interesting, eh?'

'Certainly wicked. You know, everyone has their own talents. My sister Ellie is a talented dancer, my sister Alex is a talented vet—'

'And you're a talented linguist.'

'Oh, that! That's just earning a living. No, my real talent, the thing at which I'm practically a genius, is getting my own way.'

'Now you really interest me.'

'It can always be done, if you know how to go about it.'

'Cunning?'

'Certainly. Cunning, devious, manipulative, wicked—whatever it takes.'

'Is that the real reason you broke off your career to go travelling?'

'In one sense. I wanted to find another world, and I'm finding it. That's the way to live. Know what you want, and don't stop until you get it.' She raised her glass to him. 'I guess there's probably a lot of interesting wickedness in your own life.'

He assumed a shocked air.

'Me? No time for it. I'm far too busy earning a respectable living, I assure you.'

'Right. I'll believe you. Thousands wouldn't.'

He grinned. 'You do me an injustice.'

'No, I don't. Any man who proclaims himself respectable needs to be treated with suspicion.'

'I protest—'

'Don't bother because I won't believe a word you say.'

They plunged into a light-hearted argument with much vigour on both sides, but also much laughter. When she looked at her watch she was amazed to see how much time had passed. She had a strange sense of being mentally at one with him. Almost like a brother.

But the next moment he turned his head so that she saw his profile against the glittering light from the fountain. Not brotherly, she thought. Disconcertingly attractive in a way that eclipsed other men, even Don. Or perhaps especially Don. But definitely not brotherly.

She remembered the first time she and Don had ventured beyond kisses, both eager to explore. But something had been missing, she knew that now.

'Are you all right?' Lucio asked.

'Yes, fine.'

'Sure? You seemed as if something had disturbed you.'

'No, I guess I'm just a bit hungry.'

'They do great snacks here. I'll get the menu.'

'I'll just have whatever you're having.'

He ordered spicy rolls and they sat eating contentedly.

'Why are you looking at me like that?' she asked.

'Just trying to solve the mystery. You don't strike me as the kind of woman who goes along with whatever the man orders.'

'Dead right, I'm not. But this is new territory for me, and I'm learning something fresh all the time.'

'So I'm part of the exploration?'

'Definitely. I like to find something unexpected. Don't you?'

'I sometimes think my life has had too much that's unexpected. You need time to get used to things.'

She hoped he would expand on that. She was beginning to be intrigued by everything he said. But before she could speak there was an excited cry as more crowds surged into the piazza, eager to toss coins into the water. For a while they both sat watching them.

'It's the age of science,' she reflected. 'We're all supposed to be so reasonable. Yet people still come here to toss coins and make wishes.'

'Perhaps they're right,' he said. 'Being too reasonable can be dangerous. Making a wish might free you from that danger.'

'But there are always other dangers lurking,' she mused. 'What to do about them?'

'Then you have to decide which ones to confront and which to flee,' he said.

She nodded. 'That way lies wisdom. And freedom.'

'And freedom matters to you more than anything, doesn't it?' he asked.

'Yes, but you must know what it really means. You think you're free, but then something happens, and suddenly it looks more like isolation.'

A sudden bleakness in her voice on the last word caught his attention.

'Tell me,' he said gently.

'I thought I knew my family. An older brother and sister who were twins, a younger sister, but then it turns out that there's been a big family secret all along. It began to come out and—' she gave a sigh '—I was the last one to know. I've always been closest to Matt, even though he can be so distant sometimes, but now it's like I'm not really part of the family. Just an outsider, in nobody's confidence.'

'You spoke of nobody caring. Nobody at all? What about outside the family?'

She grimaced. 'Yes, there was someone. We were moving slowly but I thought we'd get there in time. Well, I'm an outsider there, too. It feels like wandering in a desert.'

She checked herself there. She hadn't meant to confide her desert fantasy, for fear of sounding paranoid, but he seemed to understand so much that it had come out naturally.

'I know the feeling,' he said, 'but a desert can be a friendly place. There's no one there to hurt you.'

'It's true there are no enemies there,' she said. 'But no friends either, nobody who cares about you.'

'You wouldn't want to be there for ever,' he agreed. 'But for a while it can be a place to rest and recruit your strength. Then one day you can come back and sock 'em on the jaw.'

She longed to ask him what events and instincts lay behind that thought. All around her doors and windows seemed to be flying open, revealing mysterious roads leading to mists and beyond, to more mysteries, tempting her forward.

But could it be right to indulge her confusions with a stranger?

Then she saw him looking at her, and something in his eyes was like a hand held out in understanding.

Why not?

What harm could come of it?

'I guess my real problem is that I'm no longer quite sure who I am,' she said.

He nodded. 'That can happen easily, and it's scary.'

'Yes, it is. With Don I always felt that I was the one in charge of our relationship, but then I found I wasn't. Oh, dear, I suppose that makes me sound like a managing female.'

'Sometimes that's what a man needs to bring out the best of him,' he said.

'Did that happen to you?'

'No, she wasn't "managing" enough. If she had been, she might have bound me to her in time to save us both.' He added quickly, 'Go on telling me about you.'

Now a connection had been established it was easy to talk. Neither of them went into much detail, but the sense of being two souls adrift was a bond. It was a good feeling and she was happy to yield to it.

'What happened to your gift for getting your own way?' he asked at last.

'I guess it failed me. I didn't say it worked all the time. You have to seize the chance, but sometimes the chance can't be seized.'

A cheer that went up from the fountain made them both look there.

'More coins, more wishes,' he said.

'Aren't they supposed to wish for a return to Rome?' she asked.

'Yes, but they always add another one, usually about a lover.'

'I'd like to go closer.'

As they neared the water they could see a man tossing in coins by the dozen, then closing his eyes and muttering fiercely.

'What's he wishing for?' Charlotte asked.

'My guess is he wants his lady-love to appear out of the blue, and tell him he's forgiven. When a guy's as desperate as that it's pretty bad.'

Then the incredible happened. A female hand tapped the young man on the shoulder, he turned, gave a shout of joy and embraced her.

'You came,' he bellowed. 'She came, everyone. She's here.'

'You see, it works,' someone shouted. 'Everyone toss a coin and make a wish.'

Laughing, Charlotte took two coins from her bag and threw one in, crying, 'Bring me back to Rome.'

'That's not enough,' Lucio said. 'Now you must wish that Don will come back.'

'Too late for that. We're not right for each other. I know that now. But what about you? Your lady might arrive and decide to "manage" you, after all, since it's so obviously what you want.'

But he shook his head. 'She's gone to a place from which she'll never return.'

'Oh, I'm so sorry. Did it happen very recently?'

'No,' he said softly. 'It was a hundred thousand years ago.'

She nodded, understanding that time, whether long or short, could make no difference to some situations. But another thought danced through her mind so fleetingly that she was barely aware of it. Another woman had stood between them, but no longer. Suddenly she had vanished, leaving only questions behind.

Impulsively she reached out and laid a hand on his cheek.

'Hey, you two, that's not good enough,' came an exultant cry from nearby. 'This is the fountain of love. Look around you.'

Everywhere couples were in each other's arms, some hugging fondly, some kissing passionately. Lucio gazed into her face for only a moment before drawing her close.

'I guess they feel we're letting the side down,' he said.

'And we can't have that, can we?' she agreed.

The feel of his lips on hers was passionate yet comforting, confirming her sensation that she was in the right place with the right person.

'I'm glad I met you,' he whispered against her mouth.

'I'm glad, too.'

They walked slowly back along the Via Vittorio Veneto. Neither spoke until they reached the hotel and he said, 'Let me take you up to your room.'

She could have bid him goodnight there and then, but she didn't. She knew now that as the evening passed the decision had been slowly building inside her. What she was going to do was right, and whatever might come of it, she was resolved.

When they reached her room he waited while she opened the door. Then he took a step back, allowing her time to change her mind. But she had passed that point, and so had he. When she held out her hand he took it, followed her inside and closed the door, shutting out the world.

In the morning she awoke to find herself alone. By her bed was a scrap of paper, on which was written, 'Thank you with all my heart. Lucio.'

At breakfast she looked around but didn't see him. She realised that she didn't even know his last name.

Strangely the situation did not distress her. They had been ships that passed in the night because that was what both of them had chosen, both of them needed. He'd been passionate and at the same time a gentle, considerate lover, with a mysterious gift for making her feel as though her troubles were falling away. She could go on to whatever the future held, stronger and more confident.

But gradually, a few weeks later, she discovered what the future did hold, and she realised that nothing would ever be the same. Now it mattered that she didn't know his full name. It took several hours' online research to discover that he was Lucio Constello, one of the most notable men in the business, with vineyards all over the country. But the most famous one was in Tuscany.

She'd set out to confront him, wondering how this business could possibly end, and soon she would know.

There he was, far ahead. The moment of truth had arrived, and she had no choice but to go forward.

# CHAPTER TWO

'I'M NOT imagining this, am I?' he asked slowly. 'It's really you?'

'Sure it's me,' she said lightly.

'You…here? In Tuscany? It's great but I can hardly believe it.'

'Why? There was always a chance we'd bump into each other again.'

The reference to chance was deliberate. She was determined to play it casual. There must be no hint of how frantically she'd searched for him, how much it mattered. She, who prided herself on fearing nothing, had been dreading this meeting, dreading the sight of his face when she told him her news.

She covered her feelings with a smile, a cheerful shrug. He mustn't suspect before she was ready.

'I'm flattered you even remember me,' she said.

'Oh, yes,' he murmured. 'I remember. We had a great evening. You made me laugh.'

She stayed calm, although it was hard. Was laughter all he remembered about that night?

'As you did me,' she returned brightly.

'Yes, we had a wonderful time. I'm sorry I had to leave so suddenly the next morning. You were deeply asleep and I didn't want to awaken you.'

That wasn't quite the truth. He'd been overtaken by
a desire to keep that perfect night apart, separate from
all other contacts, like a picture in a frame. It had made
him slip silently out of the room, leaving behind only
the note that gave no clue to his identity or whereabouts.
Perhaps he should be ashamed of that, but he couldn't
think of it now.

The sight of her approaching had filled him with an
overwhelming gladness. The awareness of that night was
there again, spectacular, intense. She was even more
beautiful than he remembered, and for a moment he felt
nothing but pleasure.

Then she destroyed it.

'I had to find you,' she said. 'There's something you
need to know.' She took a deep breath. 'I'm pregnant.'

'Wh-what?'

'I'm pregnant. I'm carrying your child.'

To his own horror his mind went blank. The pleasure
at seeing her, the joy at the beautiful memories, everything vanished. He had the sensation of being punched
in the face.

'Are you…sure?' he asked, barely knowing what he
said.

'Quite sure. And in case you're wondering, I don't
make a habit of doing what I did that night, so there hasn't
been anyone else. You're the father.'

'Look, I didn't mean…'

He could have cursed himself for his clumsiness but
he couldn't help it. He didn't mean—what? And what *did*
he mean? If anything.

Watching him intently, Charlotte saw the last thing in
the world she'd wanted to see. Confusion. Blank. Nothing.

A desert.

In a blinding flash her courage collapsed. Don had

rejected her, and although her heart hadn't been broken, rejection was still rejection. Now Lucio was working himself up to reject her, and she wasn't going to hang around for it.

'It's OK, it's OK,' she said with a good imitation of a cheerful laugh. 'There's no need to panic.'

'I'm not—'

'Oh, yes, you are. You're on the verge of a panic attack. Oh, poor Lucio! Did you think I was trying to trap you into marriage? Not a chance! You and me? Get real! It would never work. We'd always—well, never mind that. Just don't panic. You're completely safe from me, I promise you. I'm only here because you have the right to know. Fulfilling my citizenly duty. How about that?'

She even managed a teasing note in the last words, and had the bitter satisfaction of seeing uncertainty in his face. He was floundering. Good. Serve him right!

'So there it is,' she said. 'Now you know. If you want to talk about it you'll find me here.' She thrust a piece of paper into his hand. 'But if you don't want to, that's just fine. Goodbye, Lucio. It was nice knowing you.'

Turning on her heel she walked swiftly away, determined to escape before he could insult her with any more blank-faced confusion.

But she gave him a last chance. That was only fair. After hurrying a few hundred yards she looked back, expecting to find him watching her, even perhaps stretching out a hand. That would have made her pause to see if he followed.

But he was frozen where she'd left him, immobile, staring down at the paper in his hand. She waited for him to look up, see her, call her name.

Nothing! Damn him!

There was only one thing to do, and that was vanish. She managed this by moving sideways between the vines so that she slipped into the next alley. This she did again, then again and again until she was several alleys away from the one where she'd started. Then she began to run, and didn't stop until she reached her car. A few moments later she was speeding away from the estate.

As she fled she asked herself ironically what else she'd expected. A man who shared a woman's bed and vanished without a goodbye had sent her an unmistakable message. The woman who chose to ignore that message had nobody to blame but herself if she suffered rejection.

And it certainly was rejection. Lucio hadn't said the actual words, but only because he'd been trying to phrase them tactfully. She wouldn't hear from him again but it didn't matter. She'd told him what he had a right to know and her conscience was clear.

She thought of her family back home in the States. She'd known of her pregnancy for several weeks, but so far hadn't told them. How would they react?

Or did she know the answer, only too well? They would accept it as no more than you'd expect from Charlotte—the difficult one, unpredictable, awkward, never quite fitting in.

And the one-night stand? Well, that was just like her, wasn't it? Always ready to explore new territory, even if it might have been best left unexplored. Not that she was exactly a bad girl...

But then again, maybe she was.

She wished her brother, Matt, was here right now. Strange that they should be so close, when he was Ellie's twin, not hers. But there was something in their natures that clicked. She knew that he, too, sometimes felt adrift in a desert, and he fought it the way she did herself, with humour that was ironic and sometimes bitter. She could almost hear him now. 'Why did you bother finding this guy? He didn't even give you his last name. Doesn't that tell you something?'

*Perhaps he did tell me the name,* she thought, *I just can't remember it. It didn't matter. It was that sort of evening. All about having fun.*

But it hadn't been fun trying to track him down afterwards. The thought of applying to the hotel for information had made her shiver with shame. Instead she'd gone to an internet café and then ransacked the internet for Italian vintners until she found no less than five of them called 'Lucio.' Luckily there was a photograph that identified him, but the search had made her feel like some abandoned serving girl from a bygone era. Which didn't improve her temper any.

She'd finally identified him as Lucio Constello, one of the most successful men in the business. His wine was famous throughout the world, and he seemed to live a glamorous life, enjoying yacht trips, rubbing shoulders with celebrities, making money at every point. There were pictures of him with beautiful women, one of whom had recently ended a romance with a film producer.

'And perhaps we know why,' enthused the text. 'Just look at the way they're gazing at each other.'

But after that the starlet was never seen with him again.

One article declared that he was 'a man who really knew how to enjoy himself.' Which meant, Charlotte thought wryly, that one-night stands were a normal part of his life. Hence his disappearance and her feeling that he wouldn't be pleased to see her.

His vineyards were many, spread out over Italy, and all subject to his personal supervision. Crisis! He could be anywhere. But an article revealed that he usually spent

May in Tuscany at the Vigneto Constanza. There was time to catch him.

At the same time a perverse inner voice argued that there was no need to contact him at all. What did this baby really have to do with Lucio? Forget him. He belonged in the past.

But her mother's voice seemed to flit through her mind. It was weeks since she'd learned the truth of how Fenella had led Cedric Patterson into accepting Clay Calhoun's twins as his own, yet still the deception haunted her. No matter how much she tried to defend her mother she knew that she herself must be honest. So she would write to Lucio.

But somehow the letter wouldn't get itself written. Whatever tone she adopted was the wrong one. Too needy. Too hopeful. Too chilly. Too indifferent.

So she'd headed for Tuscany, checking into a hotel in the picturesque old city of Florence, and hiring a car from the hotel for the rest of the journey. For part of the way a map was useful, but when she grew nearer she asked directions. Everyone could point the way. The Vigneto Constanza was known and respected for miles around, clearly a source of welcome employment which was probably why they called the house a *palazzo*, she thought.

But she changed her mind when she saw the building, which was certainly a palace, rearing up three floors, with an air of magnificence that suggested nobility rather than business.

As she approached a middle-aged woman came out and stood waiting on the step.

'Good morning,' she said as Charlotte got out of the car. 'I'm Elizabetta, the housekeeper. Can I help you?'

'I'm here to see Signor Constello.'

'I'm afraid he's not here,' Elizabetta said.

Charlotte gave a sharp breath. He'd vanished. She'd pursued him for nothing. Suddenly she was in the desert again.

But then Elizabetta added, 'Not just now anyway. He's gone out inspecting the vines on the far side of the estate.'

'But he is…coming back?'

'Well, it's a big estate. He won't be home until very late, and sometimes he stays the night with one of his workers who lives on the far side.'

'I need to see him today. Can you tell me where he'll be?'

A few minutes later she headed off in what she hoped was the right direction. The sheer size of the grape fields was stunning—acre after acre, filled with long straight lines that seemed to stretch into infinity. She wouldn't have been surprised to discover that she'd arrived on a strange planet, and Lucio wasn't here at all.

'Stop being fanciful,' she told herself sternly. 'There he is in the distance. Everything's going to be all right.'

Instead nothing was all right. His response had been so bleak that she'd fled after a few minutes, and was now back in Florence, pacing the floor of her hotel room.

The paper she'd left him had contained both the hotel details and the number of her cell phone. He would call her soon, and they would settle it. But as time passed with no call, she faced the fact that she was alone again.

Another desert.

As the light faded she sat at the window, looking out at the old city. Her room overlooked the beautiful river Arno, with a clear view of the Ponte Vecchio, 'the old bridge,' which had stood there for over a thousand years. It was lined with shops on both sides, at one time a common Italian habit. But that convention had faded, and now the Ponte Vecchio was almost unique in still having them. They were lit up, dazzling and golden against the night air, flooding the water with light.

On impulse she determined to go down and explore the bridge. She would take her cell phone. Lucio could call that number if he wanted to contact her. But if he didn't, he needn't think she was going to languish here waiting for him to deign to give her his attention.

In a moment she was downstairs and out of the door, heading for the street that ran along the river. Despite the lateness of the hour she was far from alone. Couples strolled slowly, absorbed in each other or leaning over the wall to gaze at the water before turning to meet each other's eyes.

At last she reached the bridge and walked halfway across to where there was a gap in the shops and she could look out over the dazzling water. On either side of her couples murmured, pleading, suggesting, happy.

Happy, she thought. Was it really possible to be happy in love?

And what was love anyway?

Briefly she'd thought she'd discovered the answer with Don, but she knew differently now. Not just because he'd let her down, but because in one devastating night with Lucio she'd discovered something that had reduced all other experiences to nothing.

Gazing down into the shimmering water, she seemed to be back in the hotel room, hearing the sound of the door close, feeling him move close. How warm his breath had been on her face, how gladly she had drawn closer to him, raising her head to receive his kiss.

She could still feel his mouth on hers, silencing the last of her doubts. Until then the voice of reason had whispered that she mustn't do this with a man she'd only just met. It wasn't proper behaviour. But the gentle, skilful movements of his lips had conquered her. Propriety had never meant much to her. In his arms it meant nothing at all.

It was obvious that he was a ladies' man, but he'd undressed her with an air of reverent discovery that made her feel special. Of course this was merely part of his expertise, she'd guessed, but it was hard to be realistic when his eyes on her were full of astonished worship.

He'd removed her dress, but before stripping her completely he'd tossed aside his jacket and shirt. There were no lights on in the room but enough came through the window to reveal his smooth, well-shaped chest and arms. Lying beside her on the bed, he'd drawn away her slip and bra, leaving only her briefs.

Then he'd smiled.

Something in that smile had made her reach for him and begin pulling at his clothes until he wore no more than she did. Now she, too, was smiling. This man was going to prove a skilful lover. Every instinct she had told her that was true.

His body was marvellous, muscular but lean and taut, hinting at strength that could bring a woman joy. Almost tentatively she slipped her fingers beneath the edge of his briefs.

Incredibly there was a question in his eyes, almost as though he was asking her even now if she had any doubts. Her reply was to tighten her grip, silently ordering him to strip naked. He obeyed and did the same for her, then stayed looking down at her, letting his fingertips drift across her breasts.

His caress was so light that he could barely be said to be touching her at all, yet the thunderous pleasure that went through her was like a storm. How could so much result from so little? she wondered frantically. Then all thought was forgotten in the delight that possessed her.

No man touched a woman so subtly without first understanding her, not just her body but traces of her heart and mind. Instinct from deep inside told her so, and everything in her responded to him. She couldn't have prevented that response even if she'd wanted to, but she didn't want to. Nothing was further from her desire than to resist him. In that magical moment she was all his, and all she wanted was to make him all hers.

Afterwards, he kissed her tenderly, stroking her hair as sleep began to claim her, and she felt herself drifting away into the sweet, warm darkness.

At the very last moment he whispered, 'You're wonderful.'

The night descended totally before she could respond, but that soft tribute lingered with her in the mysterious other universe where there was rest, peace and joy.

But when she awoke, he was gone.

The memory of the murmured words tormented her. Had she imagined them, or had he really said such a thing before abandoning her? Again and again she went over the moment, racking her brain to know whether it was true memory or only fantasy born of wishful thinking. The search nearly drove her crazy, but she found no answer.

In the weeks that followed she'd known that she could have loved him if he'd given any sign of wanting her love. Instead he'd rejected her so brutally that she'd come close to hating him.

It was cruelly ironic that her two encounters with Lucio had both been under circumstances that suggested romance. First the Trevi Fountain where lovers laughingly gambled on their love, and where she'd been tempted to gamble beyond the boundaries of both love and sense. Now she was in another city so enchanting that it might have been designed for lovers. But instead of revelling in the company of a chosen man she was alone again. Unwanted. Looking in from the outside, as so many times before in her life.

But enough was enough. This was the last time she would stand outside the magic circle, longing for a signal from within; the last time she would wait for a man to make up his mind. *Her* mind was made up, and he could live with it.

She almost ran back to the hotel. At the desk she stopped just long enough to ask, 'Any message for me? No? Right. I'm checking out in half an hour. Kindly have my bill ready.'

In her room she hurled things into the suitcase, anxious to lose no time now the decision was made. Her next step was vague. A taxi from the hotel to the railway station, and jump on the next train to—? Anywhere would do, as long as it was away from here.

At the desk the bill was ready. It took only a moment to pay it, seize up her baggage and head for the door. Outside she raised her hand to a taxi on the far side of the road, which immediately headed for her.

'Where to?' the driver called.

'Railway station,' she called back.

'No,' said a voice close by. Then a hand came out of the darkness to take her arm, and the same voice said, 'Thank goodness I arrived in time.'

She jerked her head up to see Lucio.

'Let me go,' she demanded.

'Not yet. First we must talk. Charlotte, neither of us should make hasty decisions. Can't you see that?' He laid his other hand on her shoulder. His touch was gentle but firm. 'You're not being fair, vanishing like this,' he said. 'I trusted you. Perhaps I shouldn't have done.'

'Perhaps *I* shouldn't have trusted *you*. I gave you the chance. I told you what had happened. You could have done anything but you chose to do nothing. Fine! I get the message.'

'There's no message. I was confused, that's all. It took me a while to get my head around it, but I thought at least you'd stay one night—give me a few hours to think.'

'What is there to think about?' she demanded passionately. 'The baby's here, inside me, waiting to be born and change everything. You're either for that or against it.'

He made a wry face. 'You really don't understand much about human weakness, do you? I didn't jump to your command at once, so you thought you'd make me sorry.'

'That's nonsense,' she said, but she knew a moment's discomfort at how close he'd come.

'I don't think so. Look, let's put this behind us. We have too much at stake to risk it with a quarrel.' He addressed the driver. 'Leave the bags. Here.'

He held out a wad of cash which the driver pocketed and fled.

'You've got a cheek,' she said indignantly.

'Not really. I'm taking a big gamble. I didn't anticipate you leaving without giving me a fair chance. I thought you'd wait for me to pull my thoughts together.'

'All right, maybe I was a bit hasty,' she said reluctantly.

'I wonder if it will always be like that with us, each of us going in opposite directions.'

'I think that sounds an excellent idea,' she said. 'If I had any sense I'd go in another direction right this minute.'

'But if you had any sense,' he replied wryly, 'you wouldn't have wasted time on me in the first place.'

'I guess you're right.'

'But since you did, and since the world has changed, isn't it time we talked to each other properly. There's a little café just along there where we can have peace. Will you come with me?'

She hesitated only a moment before taking his hand and saying, 'Yes. I think perhaps I will.'

# CHAPTER THREE

AFTER dumping her bags in his car Lucio indicated the road that ran along the side of the river. 'It's not far. Just a quiet little place where we can get things sorted.'

But when they reached the café Charlotte backed off. Through the windows she could see tables occupied by couples, all seemingly blissful in each other's company.

Not now, she thought. An air of romance wasn't right for this discussion. She needed a businesslike atmosphere.

'It's a bit crowded,' she said. 'Let's find somewhere else.'

'No, they won't bother us,' he said, which left her with a curious feeling that he'd read her thoughts. 'This way.'

He led her to a table by a window, through which she could see the golden glow of the water, and the little boats all of which seemed to be full of adoring couples.

But this situation demanded efficiency, common sense. The last thing it needed was emotion.

Her mood had calmed. She was even aware of a little shame at how hastily she'd judged him. But it still irked her that he'd taken control. She glanced up and found him studying her with a faint smile.

'If looks could kill, I'd be a dead man,' he observed lightly.

'Unless there was some quicker way,' she replied in the same tone.

'If there was, I'm sure you'd know it.'

'Well, you've got a nerve, just taking over like that.'

'But I asked if you'd come with me. You said yes.'

'And if I'd said no, what would have happened?'

He gave a smile that made her heart turn over. 'I'd probably have taken the advice you offered me in Rome.'

'I gave you advice?'

'As I recall your exact words were, "Know what you want and don't stop until you get it". Impressive advice. I know what I want and, well—' He spread his hands in an expressive gesture.

'So you think you can do what you like and I can't complain because I put you up to it.'

'That's a great way of putting it. I couldn't have done better myself.'

'I—you—'

'Ah, waiter, a bottle of my usual wine, and sparkling water for the lady.'

'And suppose I would have liked wine,' she demanded when they were alone.

'Not for the next few months. It wouldn't be good for you or the person you're carrying.'

His use of the word *person* startled her. How many men saw an unborn child as a person, still less when it had been conceived only a few weeks ago? She knew one woman whose husband referred to 'that thing inside you'. But to Lucio this was already a person. Instinctively she laid a hand over her stomach.

Then she looked up to find him watching her. He nodded. After a moment she nodded back.

Now she'd had a chance to get her thoughts in order

she found her brief hostility dying. She could even appreciate his methods.

When the waiter returned with the drinks Lucio ordered a snack, again without consulting her. But it was hard to take offence when he was ordering the same things she'd enjoyed in the outdoor café at the Trevi Fountain, a few weeks and a thousand lifetimes ago. How had he remembered her taste so perfectly? The discovery made him look slightly different.

Studying him, she discovered another change. The man in Rome had been a flamboyant playboy, handsome, elegantly dressed, ready to relish whatever pleasures came his way. The man in the vineyard that afternoon had worn dark jeans and a sweater, suitable for hard work on the land.

The man sitting here now wore the same clothes but his eyes were tense. His manner was calm, even apparently light-hearted, but there was something else behind it. She sensed apprehension in him, but why was he nervous? Of her? The situation? Himself?

When the waiter had gone he turned back to her.

'I'm sorry for the way this happened, but I never dreamed you'd just leave like that.'

'And I thought my leaving was what you wanted. Your silence seemed rather significant.'

'My silence was the silence of a man who's been knocked sideways and was trying to get his head together. You tell me something earth-shattering, then you vanish into thin air, and I'm supposed to just shrug?'

'I guess I thought you were more sophisticated than this.'

'What you thought was that this kind of thing happened to me every day, didn't you?'

'Nonsense,' she said uncomfortably.

'Be honest, admit it.'

'How can I? I don't know the first thing about you.'

'Nor I about you,' he said wryly. 'That's our problem, isn't it? We've done it all back to front. Most people get to know a little about each other before they—well, anyway, we skipped that bit and now everything's different.

'I didn't contact you earlier because I was in a state of shock. When I'd pulled myself together I picked up the phone. Then I put it down again. I didn't know what to say, but I had to see you. I had to know how you feel about what's happened. Tell me frankly, Charlotte, do you want this baby?'

Aghast, she glared at him. 'What are you saying? Of course I want it. Are you daring to suggest that I get rid of it? I'd never do that.'

'No, I didn't mean—it's just—' He seemed to struggle for the right words. 'Do you really want the child or are you merely making the best of it?'

She drew a slow breath. 'I don't know. I've never thought of it like that. From the moment I knew, it felt inevitable, as though the decision had been taken out of my hands.'

He nodded. 'That can be a strange feeling, sometimes bad but sometimes good. You get used to planning life, but then suddenly life makes the plans and orders you to follow them.'

'Oh, yes,' she murmured. 'I know exactly what you mean.'

'And maybe it can be better that way. It can save a lot of trouble.'

'You'll have me believing that you're a fatalist.'

'Perhaps,' he said quietly. 'Things happen, and when you think you've come to terms with it something else happens and you have to start the whole process again.'

'Yes,' she murmured. 'Nothing is ever really the way we thought it was, is it?'

'No,' he said. 'That's true, and somehow we have to find our way through the maze.'

She turned to meet his eyes and saw in them a confusion that matched her own.

'I can hardly believe you're pregnant,' he said. 'You look as slim as ever.'

'I'm two and a half months gone. That's too early for it to show, but it'll start soon.'

'When did you know?'

'A few weeks ago. I was late, and when I checked—' she shrugged '—that was it.'

She waited for him to demand why she hadn't approached him sooner, but he sat in silence. She was glad. It would have been hard for her to describe the turmoil of emotions that had stormed through her in the first days after the discovery. They had finally calmed, but she'd found herself in limbo, uncertain what to do next.

When she'd discovered his likely location she hadn't headed straight there. Her mind seemed to be in denial, refusing to believe she was really pregnant. Any day now it would turn out to be a mistake. She'd continued her trip around Italy, heading back south but avoiding Rome and going right down to Messina, then crossing the water to the island of Sicily, where she spent a month before returning north.

At last she faced the truth. She was carrying Lucio's child. So she went to find him, telling herself she was ready for anything. But his response, or lack of it, had stunned her. Now here she was, wishing she was anywhere else on earth.

From the river below came the sound of a young woman screaming with laughter. Glancing down Charlotte saw the girl fooling blissfully with her lover before they vanished under the bridge. Lucio watched her, noticing how the glittering yellow burnished her face, so that for a moment she looked not like a woman but like a golden figurine, enticing, mysterious, capable of being all things to all men, or nothing to any man.

'So tell me what you're thinking,' he said. 'Tell me how it looks to you, and where you see the path leading.'

'I can't answer that. I see a dozen paths leading in different directions, and I won't know which one is the right one until we've talked.'

'If I hadn't turned up just now where were you headed?'

She shrugged.

'Home?' he persisted. 'To New York?' He searched her face. 'You don't know, do you?'

'Does it matter?'

'What about your family? How do they feel about it?'

'I haven't told them yet.'

He stared. 'What, nothing?'

'Nothing.'

'I see.' He sat in silence for a moment and when he spoke again his tone was gentle.

'When we talked in Rome you said there was a secret that you'd been the last to know, and you felt as though you weren't really part of the family any more. You still feel like that?'

'I guess so.'

'All these weeks you've had nobody to confide in?'

'It wouldn't be a good time.'

The thought of her family had made her flinch. So much was going on there already—the truth about Matt and Ellie's paternity, her feeling of isolation, her uncertainty about what a family really meant—she couldn't confide in them until she'd made up her own mind. She didn't even tell Matt. She'd always felt close to him before, but not now.

'So there isn't anybody—?' Lucio ventured slowly.

'Don't you dare start feeling sorry for me,' she flashed. 'I can look after myself.'

'Will you stop taking offence at every word? You don't have to defend yourself against me. If you'd just given me a chance this afternoon—'

'All right, I shouldn't have dashed off the way I did,' she admitted. 'But you looked so horrified….'

'Not horrified,' he corrected her gently. 'Just taken by surprise. It's never happened to me before, and it was the last thing I expected.' He made a wry face. 'I just didn't feel I could cope. I guess my cowardly side came to the surface.'

'But there's no need for you to feel like that,' she said. 'You don't have to have anything to do with this baby. I told you because you had a right to know, but I'm not expecting anything from you—'

She stopped, dismayed at his sudden frozen expression.

'Thanks,' he said harshly. 'You couldn't have showed your contempt for me more clearly than that.'

'But I didn't—I don't know what you—'

'You're carrying my child but you don't expect anything from me. That says everything, doesn't it? In your eyes I'm incapable of rising to the occasion, fulfilling my obligations. In other words, a total zero.'

'I didn't mean it like that. I just didn't want you to feel I was putting pressure on you.'

'Doesn't it occur to you that there ought to be a certain amount of pressure on a man who's fathered a child?'

'Well, like you said, we don't know each other very well.'

The words *Except in one way* seemed to vibrate in the air around them.

Seeing this tense, sharp-tempered man, she found it strange to recall the charismatic lover who'd lured her into his arms that night in Rome. How he'd laughed as they stood by the fountain, tossing in coins, challenging her to make two wishes—the conventional one about returning to Rome, and another one from her heart. She'd laughed too, closing her eyes and moving her lips silently, refusing to tell him what she'd asked for.

'Let's see if I can guess,' he'd said.

'You never will.'

That was true, for there had been no second wish. She had so many things to wish for, and no time to think about them. So she'd merely moved her lips without meaning, as part of the game.

She'd teased him all the way into her bedroom and the merriment had lasted as they undressed each other. They didn't switch on the light, needing only the glow that came through the windows, with its mysterious half shadows. His body had been just as she'd expected, slim and vigorous, not heavily muscular but full of taut strength.

Everything about their encounter had been fun: it was scandalous, immoral, something no decent girl would ever do, but she enjoyed it all the more for the sense of thrilling rebellion it gave her. No pretence, no elaborate courtesy, no bowing to convention. Just sheer lusty pleasure.

His admiration had been half the enjoyment. In the glow of success she had soared above the world, but now had come the inevitable crash landing, and the two of them stranded together.

She looked around the café, trying to get her bearings. It was hard because there were lovers everywhere, as though this part of Florence had been made for them and nobody else. Glancing at Lucio she saw him watching the couples with an expression on his face that made her draw a sharp breath. Gone was the irony, the air of control that seemed to permeate everything else that he did. In its place was a haunted look, as though his heart was yearning back to a source of sadness from which he could never be entirely free.

She looked away quickly. Something warned her that he would hate to know she'd seen that revealing expression.

One couple in particular caught her attention. They were deep in conversation, with the girl urgently explaining something to the young man. Suddenly he burst into a loud crow of joy, pointing to her stomach. She nodded, seizing his hand and drawing it against her waist. Then they threw themselves into each other's arms.

That was how it should be, Charlotte thought. Not like this.

'No prizes for guessing what she told him,' Lucio observed wryly.

'I suppose not.'

He seemed to become suddenly decisive. 'All right, let's see if we can agree on something.'

Here it was, she thought. He was going to offer her a financial settlement, and she was going to hate him for it.

'I've been doing a lot of thinking since this afternoon,' he said. 'And one thing's clear to me. You mustn't be alone. I want you to come and stay with me.'

She frowned. 'You mean—?'

'At my home. I think you'll like it there.'

Seeing in her face that she was astonished he added,

'You don't have to decide now. Stay for a while, decide how you feel, then we'll talk and you'll make your decision.'

Dumbfounded, she stared at him. Whatever she'd expected it wasn't this.

'Please, Charlotte. You can't just go off into the distance and vanish. I want you where I can look after you and our child.'

She drew a shaky breath. Of all he'd said, three words stood out.

*I want you.*

To be wanted, looked after. When had that last happened to her?

'You surely understand that?' Lucio said.

'Yes, I—I guess I'm like you. I need time to get my head round it.'

'But what's difficult? We're having a child together. That makes us a family. At the very least we should give it a try, see if it can be made to work.'

'Well, yes, I suppose so….'

'Good. Then we're agreed. Nice to get it settled. Shall we go?'

'Yes,' she said slowly, taking the hand he held out to her, and letting him draw her to her feet.

The die was cast. She had no intention of leaving him now.

'Are you all right?' he asked as they stepped out into the street.

'Yes—yes, everything's all right.'

He led her to where he'd parked the car and ushered her into the front passenger seat. In a few moments they were heading out of Florence and on the road that led the twenty miles to the estate.

There was a full moon, casting its glow over the hills

of Tuscany, and holding her spellbound by the beauty. Lucio didn't speak and she was glad because she needed time to understand what had happened.

*I want you.*

Three simple words that had made it impossible for her to leave, at least for the moment. Later, things might be different, but for now she had nowhere else to go, and nobody else who wanted her.

With a few miles to go Lucio pulled in at the side of the road and made a call on his cell phone.

'Mamma? We'll be there in a few minutes…. Fine…. Thank you!'

As he started up the engine and drove on he said, 'Fiorella isn't actually my mother. She and her husband, Roberto, were the owners of the estate when I arrived here twelve years ago. I worked for them, we grew close, and I nearly married their daughter, Maria. But she died, and Roberto followed her soon after, leaving the estate to me.'

'But shouldn't he have left it to his wife?' Charlotte asked.

'Don't worry, I didn't steal her inheritance. He left her a fortune in money. She could go anywhere, do anything, but she chooses to live here because it's where she was happy. She's been like a mother to me, and I'm glad to have her.'

Her head was in a whirl at these revelations. Lucio had been engaged to Fiorella's daughter. How would she feel at the arrival of a woman carrying Lucio's child, a child that in another life would have been her own grandchild? At the very least she would regard Charlotte as an interloper.

'You should have told me this before,' she said.

'Why? She wants to meet you.'

'But it's an impossible situation. Her daughter—you—however can this be happening?'

'Charlotte, please, I know it's difficult, but don't blame me. You've known about this pregnancy for weeks, but you sprang it on me without warning. I had to make decisions very quickly, and if I was clumsy I'm sorry. Don't look daggers at me.'

Since his eyes were fixed on the road he couldn't see the daggers, but he'd known by instinct. She ground her teeth.

What did Fiorella know about her? What had Lucio said? What had Elizabetta, the housekeeper, said after she'd arrived, asking for Lucio, earlier that day?

In the distance she could see a palatial house, standing high on a hill and well lit so that she could recognise it as the one she'd visited. As they neared she could see two women standing just outside the front door. One of them was Elizabetta and the other must be Fiorella.

The two women were totally still as the car drew up. Only when Lucio opened Charlotte's door and handed her out did they come forward.

'This is Charlotte,' he said. 'She's come to stay with us.'

Clearly neither of them needed to ask what he meant. Lucio had prepared the ground well. Elizabetta smiled and nodded, but Fiorella astonished Charlotte by opening her arms

'You are welcome in this house,' she said.

Charlotte's head spun. She'd been prepared for courtesy, but not this show of warmth from a woman whose daughter Lucio had once planned to marry. It was Maria who should have borne his children, which surely made her an interloper.

She managed to thank Fiorella calmly, and the two

women ushered her into the house while Lucio returned to the car for her bags.

'A room has been prepared for you,' Fiorella said. 'And some food will be brought to you. Tomorrow we will all eat together, but tonight I think you are tired and need to sleep soon.'

She was right, and Charlotte thanked her for her consideration. Secretly she guessed that there was another reason. Now that she'd set eyes on her, Fiorella wanted to take Lucio aside and demand more answers. And she herself would be glad to talk to him privately.

He led the way up a flight of stairs, so grandiose that they confirmed her impression that this was more of a palace than a farmhouse. Then it was down a wide corridor lined with pictures, until they came to a door.

'This is your room,' Lucio said, leading the way in and standing back for her to see.

It was a splendid place, large and extravagantly furnished, with a double bed that had clearly been freshly made up, and a door that led to a private bathroom.

'This is kept for our most honoured guests,' Lucio said. 'I think you'll be comfortable here.'

'I'm sure I will be,' she said politely.

Fiorella appeared, followed by Elizabetta pushing a table on wheels, laden with a choice of food, fruit juice and coffee.

'Have a good night's sleep,' Fiorella said. 'And we will get to know each other tomorrow. Would you like Elizabetta to unpack your bags?'

'No, thank you,' Charlotte said quickly.

She wasn't sure why she refused. But while she was still learning about this place and the people in it some instinct warned her to stay on guard.

'Right, we'll leave you alone to get settled,' Lucio said. 'Go to bed soon. It's late.'

She would have preferred him to stay, but of course he must sort out final details with Fiorella. He would come to her later.

She ate the supper, which had clearly been created by someone who knew her tastes, meaning that Lucio had been at work here, too. Then she unpacked, hung up her clothes in the elegant wardrobes and took a shower. It felt wonderful. When she stepped out her flesh was singing and she felt better physically than she had for some time.

What to wear to greet Lucio when he came? Nothing seductive. That would send out too obvious a message. The nightdress she chose was silk but not seductively low-cut. Some women would have called it boring. Charlotte called it useful. They could talk again, but this time it would be different. She no longer felt the antagonism he'd provoked in her earlier. Tonight would decide the future, and suddenly that future looked brighter than it had for months.

It was only a few hours since she'd arrived at the estate, a confident woman, certain that she knew who and what she was. She would explain the facts to Lucio, they would make sensible arrangements and that would be that.

But nothing had worked out as she planned, and now here she was, in unknown territory. She knew there was much to make her grateful. Where she might have found hostility she was treated as an 'honoured guest'. Lucio wanted their child, and was set on being a good father, which made him better than many men. But he was focused on the baby, not herself. What would happen between the two of them was something only time would tell.

She threw herself down on the bed, staring into space.

One question danced through her mind. How much had Maria meant to him? How much did her memory mean to him now? He'd spoken of her without apparent emotion, but that might have been mere courtesy towards herself. Or perhaps they had planned no more than a marriage of convenience.

Surely that wasn't important. How could it matter to her?

Yet, disconcertingly, it did.

*Face it,* she thought. *He's attractive. You thought so from the first moment in Rome, otherwise things wouldn't have happened as they did. What was it someone used to say to me?* 'When you've made a decision, have the guts to live with the result.' *I made a decision, and this is the result. Perhaps even a happy one.*

*We could even fall in love. I'm not in love with him now, but I know I could be. But isn't that a kind of love already? Well, it'll be interesting finding out.*

She smiled to herself.

*And I could win him. Couldn't I?*

*I'll know when I see him tonight. He'll be here soon.*

But hours passed and Lucio did not appear.

# CHAPTER FOUR

FROM his bedroom window Lucio could see the window of Charlotte's room. The blinds were drawn but he could make out her shadow moving back and forth against the light, until finally the light was extinguished.

He went to bed, thinking about her, lying alone in the darkness, just as he was himself. Was she struggling with confusion? Did they have that, too, in common?

He wasn't proud of himself. His reaction to her news had been fear so intense that at first it had held him frozen. After she'd left he'd spent hours walking back and forth through the alleys of vines trying to believe it, trying not to believe it, trying to decide how he felt. Failing in everything.

But as the hours passed he'd come to a decision. Life had offered him something to hold on to, something that could have meaning. A drowning man who saw a life belt within his grasp might have felt as he did then.

Looking back to the start of the day he marvelled at how clear and settled his life had seemed, and how quickly that illusion had vanished into nothing.

But that was how it had always been.

His childhood in Sicily had been contented, even sometimes happy, although he'd always sensed that his parents meant more to each other than he meant to either of them. This troubled him little at the time. It even gave him a sense of freedom. And if there was also a faint sense of loneliness he dealt with that by refusing to admit it.

But at last he became aware that the father he adored inspired fear in others, although Lucio couldn't understand why. Why should anyone be afraid of a lawyer, no matter how successful? But he'd come to realise that Mario Constello's clients were at best dubious, at worst criminal. They were used to getting their own way by threats, if necessary channelled through their lawyer.

The discovery caused something deep in Lucio to rebel in disgust. When he challenged his father, Mario was honestly bewildered. What could possibly be wrong with dishonesty and violence if it made you rich?

After that it was only a matter of time before Lucio fled. He begged his mother to come with him but she refused. She knew the worst of her husband, but even for the sake of her son she couldn't bear to leave him.

'Mamma, he's a monster,' Lucio had protested.

'Not to me, my son. Never to me. You're so young, only seventeen. One day you will understand. You'll learn that love isn't "reasonable". It doesn't obey the commands of the brain, but only of the heart.'

'But if your heart tells you to do something that could injure you?' the boy had demanded fiercely. 'Isn't that time to heed the brain and tell the heart to be silent?'

Her answering smile had contained a world of mysterious knowledge.

'If you can do that,' she said softly, 'then you do not really love. But you will, my darling. I know you will. You are warm-hearted and generous and one day you'll know what it is to love someone beyond reason. It will hit you like a lightning bolt and nothing will be the same again. And you should be glad, for without it your life would be empty.'

To the last moment Lucio hoped that she would choose him over his father, but she had not. On the night he slipped away she'd watched him go. His last memory of his old home was her standing motionless at the window until he was out of sight.

He'd headed for the port of Messina and took a boat across the straits to the Italian mainland. From there he'd travelled north, taking jobs where he could, not earning much but living in reasonable comfort on the money his mother had given him. In Naples and Rome he spent some time simply enjoying himself, and when he reached Tuscany the last of his money had gone. Someone advised him to seek work in one of the local vineyards, and he slipped away to take a sneaky look at the Vigneto Constanza, to see what kind of work it was.

There he'd collapsed from hunger and exhaustion, and by good fortune had been discovered by Roberto Constanza, who'd taken him home.

He'd spent a week being nursed back to health by Signor Constanza's wife, Fiorella, and sixteen-year-old daughter, Maria. His abiding memory was of opening his eyes to see Maria's anxious face looking down at him.

When he'd recovered he'd gone to work in the vineyard and loved it from the first moment. Unlike the other employees he'd lived in the house, and it had become an open secret that he was regarded as the son the Constanzas had never had.

He stayed in touch with his mother, but his father cut him off. Lucio's departure, with its implied criticism, had offended him, and the only message from him said, 'You are no longer my son.' Lucio's response was, 'That suits me perfectly.'

His connection with his parents had been finally severed three years after he left them. Someone with a grudge against Mario had broken into his home and shot him. His mother, too, had died because, according to a witness, she had thrown herself between her husband and his killer.

'She could have escaped,' the witness had wept. 'Why didn't she do that?'

*Because she didn't want to live without him,* Lucio thought sadly. *Not even for my sake. In the end he was the one she chose.*

There was no inheritance. Despite his life of luxury Mario had been deeply in debt, and when everything was repaid there was nothing for his son.

'Perhaps that's really why your mother chose to die with him,' Roberto suggested gently. 'She faced a life of poverty.'

'She could have come to me,' Lucio suggested. 'I wouldn't have let my mother starve.'

'But she loved you too well to be a burden on you,' Roberto said.

But the truth, as Lucio knew in some place deep inside himself, was that she had not loved him enough. Life without her adored husband would never be worth living, even if she was cared for by a loving, generous son. For a second time she had rejected Lucio.

After that it was easier to accept Roberto and Fiorella as his parents. Looking back he sensed that that was the moment when his life here had truly begun.

The years that followed were happier than he had dared to hope. Everything about being a vintner appealed to him. He was a willing pupil, eager for whatever Roberto had to teach. From almost the beginning he had 'the eye', the mysterious instinct that told him which vines were outstanding, and which merely good. He sensed every stage of ripening, knew to the hour when the harvest should begin. Roberto, a vintner of long experience, began to listen to him.

Sweetest of all was the presence of Maria, her parents' pride and joy. A daughter so adored might have become spoiled and petulant. She was saved from that fate by the wicked, cheeky humour that infused her life, and which drew him to her.

From the first moment he'd thought her pretty and charming, but at sixteen she seemed little more than a child. For a while they were like brother and sister, scrapping, challenging each other. She was popular with the local young men and never seemed short of an escort.

Lucio, who was also popular with the opposite sex, studied her boyfriends cynically and warned her which ones to be wary of. But there was no emotion in their camaraderie.

He still relived the night when everything changed. Maria was getting ready for an evening out with a young man. He was handsome, exciting, known locally as a catch, and she was triumphant at having secured his attention.

Lucio had come home late after a hard day. He was tired, his clothes were grubby and he was looking forward to collapsing when he walked into the main room downstairs and found Maria preening herself at the mirror. Hearing him approach, she'd swung round.

'What do you think?' she demanded. 'Will I knock him sideways?'

For a moment he couldn't speak. The vision of beauty before him seemed to empty his brain. Gone was the jeans-clad kid sister with whom he shared laughter. Laughter died and enchantment took its place. It was the moment his mother had foreseen, the bolt of lightning, and everything in him rejoiced.

But she was unchanged, he was dismayed to notice. She teased and challenged him just like before, went on dates with other men and generally convinced Lucio that he'd be a fool to speak of his feelings.

And why should she want him? he asked himself bitterly. She was a rich girl and he was just one of her father's labourers, despite the privilege with which he was treated. Her escorts were similarly wealthy, arriving in expensive clothes and sweeping her off to luxurious restaurants.

He tried to cure himself. Why should he love a woman who would never love him? But nothing worked. He believed she was 'the one'.

Then one night, at a party, he'd rescued her from the unwanted attentions of the host's son, and his self-control had died. Seizing her in his arms he'd kissed her fervently, again and again.

When at last he released her he found her gazing at him with ironic amusement.

'I thought you were never going to do that,' she said.

'Maria, do you mean—?'

'Oh, you're so slow on the uptake. Come here.'

This time it was her kiss, full of the fierce urgency of a young woman who'd waited too long for this and had finally lost patience.

This time their embrace was so long that her parents came in and found them. Lucio prepared to beg them to understand, not to dismiss him from the estate. But then he saw that they were smiling with delight. They knew he was the right man for their child. Nothing else mattered.

Now Maria admitted that she'd loved him for months. The next few months were sweet and gentle as they got to know each other on a new level. Long talks went on late into the night, leaving them both with a sense of a glorious future opening up. Nobody wanted to rush things, but, even without a definite proposal, it was taken for granted that they would be together forever.

One day, while they were guests at a friend's wedding, he said, 'Do you think we could—?'

'Yes,' she said quickly. 'I really think we could.'

They were engaged.

Fiorella and Roberto were overjoyed. They didn't care that he was poor.

'You're a great vintner,' Roberto told him, adding with a wicked chuckle, 'This way I can tie you to the estate. Now I don't have to worry that you'll leave me to work for someone else.'

Then he'd roared with laughter at his own joke, not fearing to be taken seriously. His and his wife's love for their foster son was too well known to be misunderstood. The only person who meant more was Maria, and the fact that they were giving her to him told him everything.

The time that followed was so joyful that, looking back, Lucio wondered why he hadn't guessed it was bound to end terribly. Fate didn't allow anyone to enjoy such happiness for more than a brief moment. He hadn't known it then but he'd learned it since.

The wedding was to take place in autumn, when the harvest was safely in. Maria and her mother had spent a long afternoon in Tuscany choosing a wedding dress, returning home in triumph. Mario had filmed her in it. Lucio had walked in while she was parading up and down for the camera. She'd laughed and displayed herself to him, but Fiorella had screamed.

'You mustn't see her in the dress before the wedding. It's bad luck.'

'Not for us, Mamma,' Maria had said blissfully.

'Not for us,' Lucio had agreed, taking her in his arms. 'We love each other too much. We will never have bad luck.'

How tragically ironic those words had become only a week later, when Maria had crashed the car she was driving, and died from her injuries. She'd lingered for two days before finally closing her eyes. Her funeral had been held in the church where the wedding should have taken place. Lucio and her parents had attended it together, bleak-eyed, devastated.

Roberto never recovered. A year later his heart gave out and he died within hours.

'He didn't want to live after we lost Maria,' Fiorella said as they sat together late into the night. 'Everything he did was a preparation for his death.' She placed a gentle hand over Lucio's. 'Including rewriting his will.'

'Mamma, I'm so sorry about that. I didn't know he meant to leave me the estate—'

'But I knew. We talked about it first and I told him I agreed. This place needs you. He's left me money and the right to live here, so there's no need for you to worry about me.'

He'd plunged into running the estate, making such a success that the profits soared and he was able to expand magnificently. Soon he owned several more vineyards and began to spend time travelling between them. The money increased even more. His life expanded into a routine of glamour.

Sometimes he felt like two people. There was the man who gladly returned home to where Fiorella, the mother of his heart, would care for him. And there was the other man who fled the estate with its memories, so achingly sweet, so beautiful, so unbearable.

There were plenty of female entanglements in his life, but none touched his heart. He steered clear of emotional involvement, flirting with women who seemed as sophisticated and cynical as himself. Even so he sometimes blundered, and knew he'd inflicted much pain before he came to realise that the part of him that loved had died with Maria.

It was lucky that he'd met Charlotte, who seemed like himself, taking life as it came, ready to make the best of a situation. He could be honest with her. He wouldn't fall in love but neither would she. Apart from the child they would give each other strength, safety, comfortable affection, but no unrealistic dreams on either side.

The future was hopeful.

Next morning Charlotte was awoken by Elizabetta, with coffee.

'Breakfast will be served downstairs when you are ready,' she said respectfully.

'I won't keep them waiting.'

She bathed and dressed quickly. Her thoughts of the previous night had shown her where the road led—developing love with Lucio and a future based on the certainties of that love. A child. A family. A secure home. It was a pity he hadn't come to her the night before. There was so much they could have said. But she suppressed her disappointment. Time was on her side. She was singing as she got out of the shower.

She chose a blue dress that was stylish, elegant, but modest. Today was about making a good impression.

There was a knock on the door, and Lucio was standing there, smiling.

'You look wonderful,' he said.

'Thank you, kind sir,' she said, taking his arm.

'Fiorella has cooked a splendid breakfast for you,' he said, leading her downstairs. 'She's the best cook in Tuscany.'

In fact, the meal was more elaborate that she normally chose, but she appreciated that Fiorella had gone to a lot of trouble to make her welcome, and expressed much appreciation.

'Your room is comfortable?' Fiorella asked. 'If the mattress is too hard or too soft it can be changed.'

'No, it's perfect. I slept so well.'

'Good. You need to build up your strength to prepare for what lies ahead. Pregnancy is exhausting. If there is anything you want, you simply tell me.'

Lucio regarded them with a pleased smile. This must be just what he'd hoped for, Charlotte thought. She returned his smile. Just looking at his handsome appearance was a pleasure.

He was dressed as she hadn't seen him before, not expensively fashionable as on the first night, nor in workman's clothes, as she'd seen him in the vineyard.

Had that only been yesterday? she wondered. The world had changed since then.

Today he looked like a businessman, plain and efficient.

'Got a meeting this afternoon,' he explained. 'Could be a big deal at stake. But we'll have this morning to ourselves and—'

His phone rang. He greeted the caller cheerfully.

'I'm looking forward to this afternoon. There's some interesting— What's that?...Damn! All right, I'm coming now.'

He hung up, scowling. 'He's got some crisis. He didn't go into details but he sounds in a bad way.' He laid a hand on Charlotte's arm. 'Sorry.'

'Don't be,' she said. 'Business comes first.'

'Bless you.'

'You can leave everything to me,' Fiorella said. 'I shall enjoy showing Charlotte around.'

When they were alone Fiorella said, 'Now, tell me how you are feeling. Is your pregnancy going well?'

'Very well.'

'Morning sickness?'

'Mostly no.'

'How lucky you are. But you will need to be registered with a doctor, and I should like to take you to the one we use. He's in Siena, only four miles away.'

She made the call at once, and a few minutes later they were heading down the hill. As the car turned Charlotte took the chance to look back for her first real view of the palace, rearing up against the sky, a magnificent building, but not at all like the farmhouse she'd been expecting.

As they neared Siena, Fiorella explained that the doctor was an old family friend, and very happy to hear her news.

In the surgery he listened to her heart, asked her questions and nodded.

'Excellent. You're in good health. About your diet—'

'You can leave that to me, Doctor,' Fiorella said.

Siena was a beautiful, historic city. As they strolled the short distance to the restaurant Fiorella had booked for lunch, Charlotte looked around her at the ancient buildings.

'I've always wanted to come here,' she murmured.

'You'll have plenty of time now. Soon it will be time for the Palio, which we never miss.'

Charlotte had heard of the Siena Palio, a horse race and pageant that was part of the town's colourful history. She asked Fiorella eager questions until they were settled in the restaurant, where, it was clear, the table had been booked in advance.

'This place is just as beautiful as I've heard,' Charlotte enthused. 'I can't believe that incredible…'

Fiorella let her talk while the food was served, occasionally joining in with an observation.

'You know this land so well,' she said at last. 'And you speak the language fluently. Lucio told me you were taking a long trip to study Italy.'

'This country has always been my passion,' she said. 'I translate for a living, and I thought I should see the reality for myself.'

'You are obviously a very independent young woman, who makes big decisions for herself. Now I am afraid I have offended you.'

'How could you possibly have done that?'

'I practically frog-marched you off to the doctor, I had this restaurant arranged without consulting you—'

'Considering how little I know about Siena restaurants, that's just as well,' Charlotte said cheerfully.

'True, but you might complain that my family had taken you over.'

'Well, perhaps I don't mind being taken over,' Charlotte mused. 'You've welcomed me, and I'm not foolish enough to object to that.'

'Then we are friends?' Fiorella asked.

'Friends,' she said warmly. Isolated from her family back home she was doubly grateful for this welcome.

'But there is still something troubling you,' Fiorella said gently.

'Not trouble exactly. I just wonder how this must be for you. You're very kind to me, but I think how painful it must be for you. Your daughter—Lucio was going to marry her, and she died….'

'And you think I must hate you because of that?'

'I couldn't blame you. I'm having the baby that should have been hers—your grandchild.'

'But it's not the same. Lucio has told me that what has happened since Rome is a surprise to both of you. He needs the stability that you can give him. Maria was—' she hesitated '—she belonged in another life, lived in another world. Now a new world opens to both of you, and I hope to be part of it, because to me he is my son.'

It was pleasantly said, and there was kindness in the older woman's eyes as she squeezed Charlotte's hand. Charlotte supposed she should be glad, since this meant Fiorella could offer her friendship. But what if she won Lucio's heart—would there be trouble looming? And it was his heart that she was determined to win.

# CHAPTER FIVE

ON THE way home Fiorella said, 'I wonder if he's finished with Enrico Miroza yet. That's the man who called this morning.'

'Enrico Miroza?' Charlotte echoed. 'Not *the* Enrico Miroza?'

'You know about him?'

'You hear his name everywhere. They say that where money's concerned he's the "big man", with a finger in every financial pie. I saw him once at a reception and he seemed so forbidding, grim and fearsome, like he ruled the world.'

'Yes, he strikes people like that, but there's another side to him. While his wife was alive he had a life of quite unnerving virtue and respectability. Then, a year after she died, he met Susanna, a greedy little gold-digger who set out to marry him for his money, and managed it. Any other man would have been wary of her, but he had very little experience of women, and he just collapsed.'

'Lucio mentioned a crisis.'

'Yes, and this is a bad time for it. Enrico is an important associate for Lucio. In a few days they'll be hosting a weekend house party in Enrico's home, for a lot of important guests. Bankers, investors, people like that.

Also, they're buying a business together, and the owner will be there.'

A few minutes later they reached the palazzo, where they saw Lucio's car parked outside.

'Good.' Fiorella sighed.

Lucio appeared and came to them quickly.

'I've brought Enrico home with me,' he said. 'He's in a bad way, and I didn't like to leave him alone.'

'But what's happened?' Fiorella asked.

'His wife's walked out on him.'

'That terrible woman!' she exclaimed. 'He's better off without her.'

'I agree, but he doesn't see it that way. He's madly in love with her no matter how badly she behaves.'

Fiorella snorted and turned to Charlotte, saying, 'This is always happening. To Susanna he's just money, money, money, and if he doesn't hand over enough she throws a tantrum.'

'This time she set her heart on a lavish set of diamonds,' Lucio said. 'When he hesitated he walked out, and I don't think it's coincidence that she picked this moment, two days before the big "do", so that he'll be humiliated before his guests. But before we go in, tell me how the two of you managed?'

'Wonderfully,' Fiorella said. 'The doctor is very pleased with our Charlotte. Now, I must go and talk to Elizabetta.'

She hurried out of the room, leaving them alone.

'Our Charlotte,' she mused. 'Did you hear that?'

'Of course. You are "our Charlotte". You're mine, but you're also hers. It's all over the estate by now, that you're keeping the family going, so in a sense you're everybody's Charlotte.'

'All over the estate? You mean people already know?'

'Good news travels fast.'

'She's so kind to me.'

'Fiorella is a matriarch in the old-fashioned sense. What counts is family. You're part of the family now. Both of you.' Smiling, he indicated her stomach.

'Yes, she as good as told me. It's so nice to be wanted and—' She checked herself, fearful of revealing too many of her innermost feelings.

'Did you notice how tactfully she left us alone?' Lucio asked. 'She knows we need time.'

He led her outside to where some seats overlooked the magnificent view down the hillside.

'I knew this was hilly country,' she said, 'but now I see it, it takes my breath away.'

'The slopes give the grapes more direct sunlight, which is one reason this area is so good for wines. At one time this part of the country housed a lot of nobility, but gradually the wine took over.'

'Is that why the house is so grand?'

'Yes, it used to belong to a count.' He grinned. 'But Enrico's home puts it in the shade. It's a real palace.'

'That's why you're having the big "do" there?'

'Right. And I'm not looking forward to it. I'll talk to some contacts and make my escape. How do you feel about coming with me? You don't have to if you think it's too soon to plunge into deep water.'

'I'd like to plunge in. Don't worry, I'll cope alone and not distract you from talking business.'

He grinned. 'Thanks.'

'Tell me about your other vineyards,' she said. 'What made you buy more?'

Lucio hesitated. To tell her that he'd been fleeing the pain of Maria's memory would have been unkind, so he merely said, 'I guess I wanted to prove myself independently, rather than just taking over another man's achievement.'

He began to describe the other estates, lingering over details to forestall more questions, until the door opened and Fiorella beckoned them.

'Time to return to duty,' Lucio said, taking her hand.

Charlotte recognised Enrico from their brief, previous encounter. Tall, thin, reserved, with a lined face and white hair, he gave the impression of a man who would never yield an inch. But his manners were perfect.

'I do apologise for my intrusion,' he said, holding her hand between both of his and speaking English.

'You don't need to. I'm delighted to meet you.'

She spoke in Italian and saw his eyes brighten with surprise.

'You know my language?'

Now he, too, spoke in Italian, and launched into a speech. At first he spoke slowly, but when she replied, speaking fast, he responded in the same way. Lost in the mental excitement, Charlotte was barely aware of Lucio watching them with a look of astonished pleasure.

'This has been a pleasure,' he said at last. 'I look forward to seeing you at the party. My friends will appreciate you, and you will enjoy yourself.'

'I look forward to it.'

Enrico stayed the night and spent dinner telling her about his home and the planned celebration. It was clear that he knew her status as Lucio's 'official lady' and the mother of his child. As Lucio had prophesied, word had spread fast.

She asked many questions, all guaranteed to show that she was up to the task. Lucio watched in silence, but seemed pleased.

Later, when Enrico had gone to his room, Fiorella

surprised Charlotte by saying in a censorious voice, 'Of course, you're not properly equipped for this occasion.'

'I think she's demonstrated that she's very well equipped,' Lucio said, astonished.

'Oh, you men! You never know what's important. So she's intelligent! So what? I'm talking about clothes. She'll need a glamorous wardrobe for this.' She took Charlotte's hand. 'Ignore him, my dear. Tomorrow we'll go into Florence and spend money.'

'Of course,' Lucio agreed. 'You must forgive my male ignorance. That hadn't occurred to me. I leave it in your hands, Mamma.'

When he'd gone Fiorella said, 'We're going to have a wonderful time tomorrow.'

Charlotte was glad, for her travelling wardrobe contained nothing that would suit such an elaborate occasion, but an imp of mischief made her say, 'Suppose I don't need any new clothes.'

'Nonsense! Of course you do!'

Laughing they went along the corridor together, and said an affectionate goodnight.

As Fiorella had prophesied, the following day was a delight. They headed for the Via de' Tornabuoni, lined with fashion boutiques. Fiorella declared that Lucio would pay for everything, and spent an amount of money that made Charlotte stare.

'The more, the better,' Fiorella declared. 'You must do him credit. There will be many such occasions, not just when you go visiting with him, but also when he brings important people home to dinner. Which reminds me that I need a couple of dresses myself for a dinner party next month.'

'Then let's start looking.' Charlotte chuckled.

They returned home in triumph, both sporting new

clothes, which they displayed to Elizabetta and the maids. Lucio, attempting to enter the room, was firmly excluded.

Two days later they set off for the Palazzo Vidani, once the home of the Dukes of Vidani, now Enrico's pride and joy.

'What did you think of him?' Lucio asked as they travelled.

'Very interesting. He seems grim and chilly, but obviously there's another side to him.'

'Yes, he's spent his life putting money first. So when he reached sixty and a fortune hunter got him in her sights he was helpless. Now she treats him like dirt, but he can't bear to get rid of her. The closest he's ever come to making a firm stand is about these diamonds which would have cost him millions.'

When they arrived Enrico greeted them at the door and personally escorted them upstairs to the luxurious ducal apartments.

'Duke Renato built this for himself and his wife in the seventeenth century,' he said, showing them around the splendid bedroom. 'She was of royal blood, so he wanted to impress her. Normally I sleep here, but tonight it's yours. I'll be in the dressing room next door.'

It was truly a room from another age. Oak panels lined the walls, which were elaborately decorated with paintings. There was also a huge fireplace, although rendered unnecessary by a discreetly located radiator. Floor-length brocade curtains framed the tall windows, and matching curtains hung around the bed which, Charlotte realised with a slight disturbance, was a double.

Clearly Enrico had assumed they slept together. He would have been aghast to learn that they had separate rooms, and that Lucio came to hers only briefly to say a chaste goodnight.

The bed was large, so they could keep a certain distance, but it was still a slight shock to discover that she had no choice in the matter. She wondered how Lucio felt about it, but when she glanced at him his face revealed nothing.

'I'll leave you to get settled in,' Enrico said. 'Tonight's the big night.'

When she saw the multitude of cars that drew up in the next hour Charlotte knew he had been right. Excitement was rising in her. If she and Lucio were to work out a future she had to be able to fit in with occasions like this, and she was confident that she could do it.

He took the first shower while she unpacked with the help of two maids who gasped with admiration as they discovered her new clothes.

'Hang them in the wardrobe,' Charlotte said. 'I want them to be a secret until the last minute.'

They nodded, understanding perfectly and giggling.

She surveyed them, wondering which one would make Lucio catch his breath. That was the one that really mattered. She didn't try to deny it to herself.

The gown that attracted her most was deep gold silk. It was elegant, sophisticated, and the bosom was just low enough to be enticing without being outrageous. When it was time to dress for the evening she slipped into the bathroom while Lucio attired himself in the bedroom. When she emerged they were both fully dressed.

It was hilarious, she thought wryly, to take such trouble not to see each other in a state of undress, when they already knew each other naked. The memory danced through her brain: Lucio, as he'd been that night, lean, vigorous, delightful.

Tonight he wore a black dinner jacket and bow tie. His hair just touched his collar, and his face was handsome and intriguing. Somehow she must spend the evening with this man without revealing how much he disturbed her. But what about him? Didn't she cause him any disturbance? Surely she must. But if so he concealed it behind perfect control.

She had a partial answer at the astonishment on his face as he approached her, and nodded.

'You'll knock them all flat,' he said. Then he dropped a light kiss on her cheek and said, 'Let's go.'

They entered the great hall down a wide staircase, and Charlotte knew at once that word had gone ahead of her. Everyone here knew what this occasion was about, and who she was.

So many people to meet. So many successful men and beautiful women, and most of those women had eyes for Lucio. The looks they cast him were the same as she'd seen in the hotel in Rome, when almost every female seemed aiming to be first with him. He could have taken any one of them to bed.

*And some of them he probably has,* she thought. *But he's with me now, so the rest of you can just back off.*

She took a deep breath and raised her head. She was ready for anything.

From the first moment she was a success. As so often the Italians warmed towards a non-Italian who'd taken the trouble to become expert in their language. They were particularly impressed by her knowledge of dialects.

Most regions of Italy had dialects vastly different from Italian. This did not apply in Tuscany, where the dialect was so like standard Italian that it was reputed to be the basis of the main language. But it was certainly true of Venice, where the *lingua Veneto* was less a dialect than an independent language that defeated most non-Venetians.

But Charlotte had been fascinated by it and, during

her visit, had managed to master a certain amount. So she was looking forward to meeting Franco Dillani, owner of the shop in Florence that Lucio and Enrico were aiming to buy.

When the moment came Signor Dillani greeted her in English.

'It is a pleasure to meet you, *signorina*.'

Beaming, she took his outstretched hand, saying, *'E mi so veramente contenta de far la vostra conoscensa, sior. Lucio me ge parla tanto de vu.'*

She had the pleasure of seeing both Lucio and Franco Dillani stare in amazement. She had spoken in Venetian, saying: 'And I am delighted to meet you, *signore*. Lucio has told me so much about you.'

'You speak all Italian languages?' he exclaimed, again in Venetian.

'No, I was just very attracted to yours,' she said.

'But that is wonderful. I am honoured.'

He immediately monopolised her, talking Venetian with great vigour until she had to protest, laughing, that he had exceeded her knowledge. Whereupon he proceeded to instruct her in *lingua Veneto*, which he enjoyed even more. By the time Lucio and Enrico converged on him for a business talk he was in the best of moods.

'How's it going?' she murmured to Lucio as the evening drew to an end.

'Wonderfully. A few more details to be settled, but the feeling is positive, thanks to you.'

'It can't be me. It must be a good deal in itself or he wouldn't be interested.'

'But tonight he's been listening as he never did before, and that's because you cast a spell on him.'

'Nonsense,' she protested, but her heart was soaring.

This was what she'd hoped for, to find a niche in his life as well as his heart.

'No, it's not nonsense. Now, let's retire for the night. You need rest. I shall want you to do a lot of this kind of thing tomorrow.'

'Your wish is my command,' she said merrily.

'You should be careful. I might take you seriously.'

Laughing they ascended the stairs together, watched by several envious pairs of eyes.

Once in their room he collected his night attire and vanished into the bathroom. Charlotte guessed that this night, however triumphant so far, would end prosaically, however much they might each hope otherwise.

Did he hope so? she wondered wistfully. Was he so much in command of himself that he could resist the temptation that teased her?

Whatever the answer, self-respect demanded that she stay in control. Her thin silk nightdress was too revealing, too obviously enticing. She covered it with a matching wrap.

There was a knock on the door that connected them to Enrico's room, and his voice called, 'May I come in?'

'Yes, of course,' she said, opening the door.

'I just wanted to say goodnight,' Enrico said. 'And to ask if you have everything you want.'

'Everything,' she said. 'It's such a lovely place.'

Lucio emerged from the bathroom and the three of them exchanged friendly goodnights, before Enrico retreated, closing the door again.

'Oh, my goodness!' Charlotte exclaimed. 'Did you see where he's sleeping? That tiny narrow bed, how spare and dismal everything is.'

'It's only meant to be a dressing room. He's making do with it tonight so that we can have his room. Still, I know what you mean.' He yawned. 'It's been a long day. I'm really looking forward to a good night's sleep.'

'So am I,' she said untruthfully.

He laid a gentle hand on her shoulder.

'You did wonderfully tonight. They all admired you.'

The movement of his hand caused the wrap to slip away to the floor. He retrieved it and laid it around her bare shoulders. His fingers barely brushed against her but suddenly Charlotte was intensely aware of every inch of her body. Every day she studied it to see if her pregnancy was becoming noticeable, but for now there was only a slight increase in the voluptuousness of her breasts and hips. It was still the same beautiful body that had entranced Lucio on the night that had changed the world. Perhaps it was even more beautiful.

And he, too, realised that. The sudden rasping sound of his breath told her that he'd become aware of her in another way. This was no longer just the mother of his child. She was the woman who'd made his spirits soar and his body vibrate.

She knew she should try to get control of herself, to subdue the thrilling impulses that invaded her. But they had always been there, she now realised, lurking in the shadows, waiting to spring out and remind her that her freedom was an illusion. Lucio's presence, or even just the sound of his voice, was enough to bring them to life, teasing, troubling, tempting.

Now she couldn't deny that ever since the first incredible night, she had wanted him again. Not just for his body's power but also its subtlety—the instinctive understanding that had told him which caresses would most delight her, the gentleness and skill that he devoted to her.

And he, too, was filled with yearning. She knew it from the way he trembled, standing so close to her. In another moment he would yield to his desires, take her in his arms and claim her in the way they both wanted. She raised her head, searching his face, and finding in it everything she longed to see. She reached up to touch him—

Then he seized her hand, holding it away from him.

'It's late,' he said. 'We both need our sleep.'

She wanted to scream that what she needed wasn't sleep. It was him, his thrilling body, his power, his passion. But that would tell him that her desire for him was greater than anything he felt for her, and her pride revolted at the thought.

'You're right,' she said. 'After all, we're here to work. Which side do you prefer?'

'This one,' he said, walking away and getting into bed on the far side.

He settled on the extreme edge, so that when she'd climbed in on her own side there was still a clear distance between them. She lay still, her face turned towards him, her whole being tense for any movement from him. But there was nothing. Lucio stayed motionless, only a slight unevenness in his breathing revealing that he was less relaxed than he pretended.

At last the sound changed, becoming quieter, more regular, telling her that the impossible had happened. Lucio, lying a few feet from her half-clad body, had fallen asleep.

It was insulting.

Only the fact that she was tired prevented her seething with indignation.

At last she, too, sank into sleep, driven more by desolation than tiredness.

She was awoken by a heavy hand on her shoulder, shaking her. Opening her eyes she saw the face of a furiously angry woman.

'I should have known,' the stranger snapped. 'I haven't been gone five minutes and already he's got another woman in my bed.'

'In your—? Are you Signora Miroza?'

'Yes, I am and you're going to regret this. And he's going to regret it even more.'

She switched on the bedside light, pointing at the far side of the bed.

It was empty.

A light beneath the door of the bathroom showed where Lucio had vanished.

'So that's where he is,' Susanna grated.

'No,' Charlotte said, pushing the woman aside. 'You've got this all wrong.'

To her relief the bathroom door opened and Lucio appeared, seemingly relaxed, smiling.

'Susanna, how nice to see you. I'm sorry that Charlotte and I are in your room, but Enrico thought you wouldn't mind.' He slipped an arm around Charlotte's shoulders, a gesture designed to make matters plain.

It worked. Susanna's jaw dropped.

'Are you two—I mean—?'

'Charlotte and I are a couple,' Lucio said. 'Enrico thought it would be nice for us to be in here.'

'But where is he? No, don't tell me. He's off in some floozy's bed, making the most of my absence.'

Charlotte lost her temper.

'No, I'll tell you where he is,' she snapped. 'And then maybe you'll stop your nonsense. Here!'

In a flash she was at the door of the dressing room, wrenching it open and switching on the light, revealing Enrico, virtuously alone in the narrow little bed.

'Nobody else,' she said firmly. 'There isn't another

door into this room and you can see he's completely alone.'

She wrenched open the wardrobe door, revealing clothes but nothing else.

Roused by the commotion Enrico had opened his eyes and was regarding them with sleepy surprise.

'Hallo,' he murmured. 'You're back.'

'I'll go now and leave you to it,' Charlotte said.

She marched out.

Lucio was waiting for her, watching her with a new light in his eyes.

'I'm beginning to realise that I've underestimated you. You can be so proper and serious when it suits you, but your other side is a cheeky imp and a warrior by turns.'

'And which one do you think is the real me?'

Slowly he shook his head.

'I'm not sure there is a real you. I think you produce whichever "you" it's useful for someone to see. You've already shown me several different faces, and I'm curious to know what surprises you still have in store for me.'

She stepped back and looked up at him, eyes bright with teasing humour.

'You'll find out—one day,' she said. 'In the meantime you'll just have to wonder.'

# CHAPTER SIX

SHE spoke lightly, watching his reaction, and was pleased to find him regarding her with new interest.

'But how long will I have to wonder?' he mused. 'I'm not a patient man.'

'Well, I know that,' she agreed.

'But it doesn't worry you?'

'Not in the least.'

He grinned. 'Think you can get the better of me, huh?'

She laughed softly. 'Think I can't?'

'I'm not foolish enough to answer that question. Like I said, I don't know how many different personalities you have hiding, ready to pop out and knock me flying.'

'Maybe I don't even know that myself. Perhaps you're the man who'll bring them out. Why don't we just wait and see?'

'I'm up for it if you are.' He nodded. 'I think life is going to become very interesting.'

'Really?' she asked, wide-eyed. 'Whatever makes you think that?'

'Either interesting or alarming. Or both.'

Before she could answer there was a noise from Enrico's dressing room.

'I wonder what's happening in there right now,' she mused.

She had an answer with unexpected speed. The door opened, revealing Susanna and Enrico, arms about each other's waists.

'Goodnight,' Susanna said majestically. 'We shall not disturb you again.'

Heads high, they crossed the room and departed. Enrico, Charlotte was fascinated to notice, looked ecstatic.

'He's got a grandiose suite down the corridor,' Lucio observed. 'They'll head for there and—whatever they feel like doing.'

'He's won this one,' Charlotte said. 'Did you ever see a man look so pleased with himself.' She gave a choke of amusement. 'Oh, goodness! His face when he first saw her.'

Lucio joined in her merriment, placing his hands on her shoulders, and suddenly the laughter died. She was no longer wearing the wrap, and the feel of his fingers against her bare skin filled her with delicious tension. The nightdress seemed flimsier than ever and she realised that his pyjama jacket was no longer respectably buttoned up high, or even buttoned up at all. It had fallen open, showing the smooth, muscular chest that she remembered.

She sensed his tension equalling her own. Also his confusion. He'd dealt with this situation earlier in the evening, but it had refused to stay dealt with. Now it was taunting him again, and he was struggling with himself, with her, but most of all with his own desire.

Good, she thought with a surge of pleasure. It would be an enjoyable battle, the herald of many. And she would always be the victor. It was time he understood that.

She leaned forward, turning her head slightly so that her cheek rested against his chest. She felt the shock go through him and the thunder of his heart, a sensation so intense that she drew back to look at his face. It was haggard, tormented, the face of a man driven by demons, far beyond his own control.

She understood that feeling. It possessed her too, giving her a powerful urge to drive the demons on, cry out to them exultantly to do their worst, because their worst was what she desperately wanted.

His caresses intensified, the fingers slipping behind her head to draw her to him so that his mouth could touch hers softly, tentatively, then urgently. Her warm breath against his face drove him on to put his arms about her, exploring, rejoicing in the feel of her flesh through the thin nightdress. He kissed her repeatedly while his hands roved over her as though this was their first time together.

And perhaps that was true. Their night in Rome had been so different, so impossible to repeat, that now they were like two strangers knowing nothing of each other except that they were flooded with desire.

He took a step towards the bed, moving slowly as though giving her time to refuse. But she was far from refusing, clinging to him frantically. He was breathing heavily, his flesh rising and falling beneath her fingers.

Then they were lying down, he was stripping away her nightdress and tossing aside the rest of his own clothes. His eyes, looking down on her, were full of fervour and his lips were touched by a smile that she had never seen before.

'You're beautiful,' he whispered. 'More beautiful than ever.'

'I don't know what you mean by that,' she said provocatively.

His fingers drifted over her, causing a storm to go through her.

'I mean this,' he said softly. 'And this.' He laid his lips

against her, moving them so skilfully that she trembled, holding him closer, whispering 'Yes, yes...'

Her hands seemed to act of their own accord, seeking, begging, demanding. Their only previous lovemaking had burned itself into her consciousness so deeply that she knew what he most enjoyed.

She closed her eyes, holding him tightly against her, desperate to relish every possible moment.

Now she could face the thought that she had never before dared to admit; that if she'd had to live the rest of her life without this man ever making love to her again, she would not have known how to endure it.

Inwardly she pleaded for this to last forever, pleasure unending, happiness without boundaries. Then, it was over, and yet not over. It would never be entirely over, she thought. Now she had everything to look forward to. Not just the sedate companionship of two people who were to have a child, but the blissful closeness of physical harmony, with its promise of a sweeter, more emotional union.

She searched his face, trying to meet his eyes for an exchange of feelings. But he turned away from her and she almost thought he shook his head. Then she saw that his eyes were closed, as though he'd retreated inside himself. With a convulsive movement he wrenched himself away from her, left the bed and strode to the window. Aghast, she followed him.

'Lucio, whatever's the matter.'

'I'm sorry,' he groaned. 'I shouldn't have done that.'

She pulled him around to face her. 'Why not?'

'Because you're carrying our child. Just the sight of you was too much for me.... Forgive me—it'll never happen again, I promise.'

She regarded him tenderly, astonished by his miserable self-blame which roused her protective instincts as nothing else in her life had ever done.

'Lucio, dear, it's all right,' she said. 'There's nothing wrong in what we've just done. I've got friends who go on enjoying each other practically until the birth. One of them has four children, all perfectly healthy. The doctor says I'm in fine shape, and as long as that's true nothing else has to change.'

'It's not just the baby,' he said sombrely. 'We've got to be careful about you. We never know what might be going to happen.'

She was about to say that he was being overly dramatic when she remembered that Maria had died suddenly, leaving him devastated. Now he went through life alert for danger and heartbreak.

She forced her own feelings to abate. It was sad that he couldn't share her delight at their union, but they had a road to travel. It was too soon to say what awaited them at the end of that road, but to her hopeful eyes it looked increasingly bright and happy.

'Don't worry about me,' she said, touching his face softly. 'I'm strong, and I'm going to give you a healthy baby.'

'Thank you. And in future I'll take better care of you. I promise.'

He spoke fervently and she loved him for his concern. Now they would fall asleep tenderly in each other's arms, the perfect way for passion to end. And there would be other moments. He might mean to keep his distance, but she knew how to change his mind.

'Everything's going to be all right,' she assured him. 'Now, let's get some sleep.'

She took his hand and tried to lead him back to the bed. But he resisted her.

'No,' he said. 'I told you I'm going to care for you, and I meant it.'

'But—'

'I can't trust myself. I've just discovered that. But you must sleep. I've tired you, and I blame myself.'

He took up her nightdress, holding it out to her at a distance and waiting while she slipped into it. Then he pulled back the covers on her side of the bed and helped her in, pushing her gently back against the pillows.

*As though I was a weakling,* she thought desperately, *when I've never felt so strong as I have tonight.*

But this wasn't the moment to protest, so she lay down and let him draw the covers over her.

She waited for him to go around to his side of the bed. Once he was in he would fall asleep, and she would be able to move quietly across the space between, slide her arms about him, rest her head on his shoulder. When he awoke to find her there he would understand that this was the truth between them. She smiled to herself.

But her smile faded as he turned away from the bed, heading for a sofa on the far side of the room.

'Lucio—' she protested.

He lay down on the sofa, his head on a cushion.

'Goodnight, Charlotte. Sleep well. I won't disturb you.'

And he wouldn't, she thought bitterly.

As she'd feared, he kept to his resolve, breathing steadily until she reckoned he must be asleep. So that was how easily he could shrug off their glorious union, she thought bitterly. That was how little it meant to him. Damn him!

From the sofa, Lucio kept his eyes on the bed where he could just make out her shape in the darkness. She lay very still, he noticed. Was she stunned by what had overtaken them? As stunned as he was himself? Or did she feel triumphant at having exposed his weakness?

When he remembered how easily he'd yielded he groaned inwardly.

He waited a long time before leaving the sofa, crossing the floor slowly and carefully to stand by the bed, watching her as she slept. At last she moved, turning over, throwing out her arms, then letting them fall back. She was murmuring something, but although he leaned closer he couldn't understand.

He reached out as if to touch her, but stayed his hand at the last minute, holding it still for several seconds before drawing it back.

He stood there for a while before returning to the sofa and lying down in the darkness.

Charlotte awoke to find herself alone. From the bathroom came the sound of Lucio singing cheerfully. After a moment he entered, fully dressed.

'Good, you're awake,' he said. 'I'll see you at breakfast.'

He departed, apparently not having noticed that the nightdress was slipping from her shoulders, revealing the beautiful swell of her breasts.

After a shower she donned a brown linen dress that was one of Fiorella's choices. It suited her perfectly, while projecting the air of sedate respectability that she guessed Fiorella had been aiming for.

She found Lucio deep in talk with Enrico, who immediately broke away to take her hand and speak warmly.

'Thank you so much, my dear Charlotte, for your help last night. I shall not forget your kind friendship.'

'I was glad to be of help. Did you and Susanna sort things out?'

'We've a way to travel yet, but we'll get there. Thanks to you. Excuse me a moment.'

Susanna had appeared, causing Enrico to hurry across to her. She was dressed in high fashion and clearly ready to flaunt herself as the hostess. She reached out to Enrico, accepting his hug as no more than her due.

'There's no fool like an old fool,' said a voice behind Charlotte.

Turning, they saw Piero, a young man-about-town they'd met the night before. He was handsome with the air of a man who would indulge himself at all costs.

'You'd think he'd have seen through her by now,' he added.

'Perhaps he doesn't want to,' Charlotte said.

'That's pretty certain. Like I say, he's a fool. Everyone knows she slept with him the night they met. That should have warned him. If a woman jumps into bed with a man she's only just met, well—we know what kind of woman she is, don't we?'

'Not necessarily,' Lucio said, clenching his hands.

'I suppose she might take you by surprise,' Charlotte mused.

'No way,' Piero declared. 'Sex on the first evening means she's after whatever she can get. Ah, I see someone I need to talk to. Bye!'

He vanished.

'Stop looking like that,' Charlotte muttered. 'Smile.'

'How can I?' Lucio ground out. 'Why aren't you insulted?'

'Why should I be? He wasn't talking about me. Unless of course you'd told him—'

'*No!*' He stared at her, incredulous and aghast. 'You're enjoying this, aren't you? How *can* you?'

'What I'm enjoying is the sight of your face. When he said it you didn't know where to look.'

'I was concerned for you. Evidently I didn't need to be.'

'That's right. My shoulders are broad. Come on, Lucio, enjoy the joke. Life's too short to get uptight about everything.'

'The sooner I get the serious business sorted out, the better,' Lucio growled. 'Then we can leave.'

'How close are you and Enrico to concluding your deal?'

'I'm not sure. He thinks the price is too high and he's holding out for a reduction.'

'Any chance that he's right?'

'None. It's a bargain because the seller wants to get rid of it quickly, and if we don't settle it now I'm afraid it'll be too late. So if Enrico delays again I'm calling it off.'

He had no need to. An hour later Enrico increased his offer, the seller accepted and the deal was concluded.

'Between you and me,' Enrico said, drawing Charlotte aside, 'I yielded out of gratitude. How could I obstruct Lucio when his wonderful lady has been such a good friend?' He added to Lucio, 'You're a lucky man. You've acquired a real asset. She'll bring you a big increase in profits.'

'That's what I'm there for.' Charlotte chuckled, and both men laughed with her.

'Now I think we'll leave,' Lucio said. 'I don't want Charlotte to get tired.'

'Of course you must look after her,' Enrico agreed.

They packed in record time and were soon on the road. Halfway home they stopped at a little village restaurant and relaxed over coffee and cakes.

'You didn't mind dashing away, did you?' Lucio asked.

'No, I think we needed to get out of there before there were any more dramas. Poor Enrico.'

'Yes, she's got him under her thumb again, and I bet she'll get her diamonds next. I don't understand how it can happen to a man like that, so powerful, so confident. He doesn't need anybody.'

'That's not true,' Charlotte mused. 'In a strange way he needs *her*.'

'How can any man need what she puts him through? You know why she came back, don't you? She was hoping to catch him with another woman, then she could divorce him and get a handsome settlement.'

'Or maybe just threaten divorce and keep him under her thumb. I think he'd pay up rather than lose her.'

'We need to rescue him from her.'

'You won't do that,' Charlotte predicted. 'She matters to him too much. And even if you could do it, it wouldn't be kind.'

'Not kind, to rescue him from a gold-digger?'

'From the only person he has to love. I heard a lot about him from other guests while we were there. He has no close family since his wife died. They had no children. He's alone in a—in a desert. And if you're stranded in a desert you often feel that you'd do anything to escape, even marry someone totally unsuitable and put up with the way they behave.'

'A desert,' he mused. 'You spoke to me of a desert on the night we met. You said you were living in one.'

'And you said it could be a good place to be,' she reminded him. 'A place to recruit your strength, and there was nobody to hurt you.'

'That's right,' he said wryly. 'It's a kind of safety.'

'Fine, if you want to be safe. But Enrico doesn't. He'd rather put up with Susanna than be safe and isolated.'

'Safe and isolated,' he murmured. 'Enrico's a brave man.'

'Yes, sometimes you have to take risks. Like we did, that night. Not that we thought of the consequences. If we had—'

'If we had you'd have run a mile from me,' he said, regarding her intently.

She gave him a faint smile. 'I'll let you know that another time.'

He had certainly never thought of the consequences, he recalled. The Charlotte he'd met in Rome had seemed so sophisticated, so adventurous and confident, that he'd simply assumed she was ready for anything.

Now he knew that what had happened that night had taken her by surprise. He, too, had been surprised, although not by the way the evening ended. That had happened to him before. What was new was the intensity of his enjoyment, not merely pleasure but a feeling of happiness as he lay in her arms.

She was wonderful. He wasn't sure if he'd told her so, although he hoped he hadn't. Safer that way.

But safe was one thing he couldn't feel in her company. She threatened his precious isolation, which he'd valued since everyone he loved had either died or betrayed him—the isolation that gave him strength and which he would cling to forever. In this mood he had fled her next morning.

But from some things there was no escape.

When they were on the road again he told her some more about his business with Enrico.

'It's just the one shop for the moment, but we'll eventually have a whole chain of wine shops in different cities. Now we've taken the first step, thanks to you.'

'Hey, I didn't do much.'

'You pulled a trigger, and it helped. And the fact that he likes you so much will also be useful in the future.'

'I'm going to be good for business, huh?' She chuckled.

'You'd better believe it. Enrico's right. Meeting you was a stroke of luck in more than one way.'

He didn't elaborate and it wasn't the time to press him, but one day soon Charlotte promised herself that she would make him enlarge on that topic.

'Did you notice that he was delighted to see us leave?' she mused. 'He wants the room back for himself and Susanna.'

'That's very cynical.'

'Sometimes cynical is the right thing to be. Aren't you ever cynical?'

'There are times when you have to be.' After a moment he added, 'And there are times when you can't afford to be.'

'I wonder which we—'

'Hey, look at that idiot!'

He braked sharply to avoid a pedestrian, then continued on the way.

Nothing was said about the night before, and soon they were on the last stretch home.

Once there he told Fiorella about the successful deal, emphasising that Charlotte had helped by winning Enrico's goodwill.

When they were alone Fiorella said triumphantly, 'You see how well you fit in here? I knew it. I'm going to cook you a special meal to celebrate.'

Charlotte couldn't help but think that Fiorella was simply trying to secure her and the child for the family, but even thinking that, it was pleasant to be treated in such a way. When she looked back on the trip she felt she had much to make her glad. If only Lucio hadn't spoiled the memory of their lovemaking by regretting it. But they were still strangers in many ways. Things would get better.

Late that night he looked into her room to say goodnight.

'The deal is set up and I'll be signing papers at the lawyer's office in a couple of days. Care to come with me?'

'I'd love to.'

'Fine. Goodnight. Sleep well.'

He departed without having come anywhere near her.

He was as good as his word, taking her to the lawyer, where they found Franco Dillani, full of good cheer at having sold the shop. With all the papers safely signed he invited them to lunch. Enrico couldn't stay but Lucio and Charlotte accepted with pleasure. Over the meal Franco was open in his admiration of Charlotte, talking Venetian with her while making the occasional apology to Lucio, who waved him aside good-humouredly.

Charlotte leaned back and just enjoyed herself. It was good to feel that she'd established a position for herself in her new life, and actually been of some real use to Lucio.

But sweeter than anything else was the knowledge that Lucio was watching her with a knowing smile on his face. His eyes, too, were full of a message that made her heart beat faster. Pleasure, admiration, satisfaction—they were all there.

But she also sensed something else, something to which she couldn't yet put a name, but which she was determined to pursue and make her very own.

Brooding on the way home, she knew the task she'd set herself wasn't going to be easy. Lucio was passionately attracted to her, yet in a strange way he feared her. What she'd seen in his eyes was a secret that he wasn't

# GET 2 BOOKS

We'd like to send you two *Harlequin® Romance* novels absolutely free. Accepting them puts you under no obligation to purchase any more books.

## HOW TO GET YOUR
## 2 FREE BOOKS AND 2 FREE GIFTS

1. Return the reply card today, and we'll send you two *Harlequin Romance* novels, absolutely free! We'll even pay the postage!

2. Accepting free books places you under no obligation to buy anything, ever. Whatever you decide, the free books and gifts are yours to keep, free!

3. We hope that after receiving your free books you'll want to remain a subscriber, but the choice is yours– to continue or cancel, any time at all!

### EXTRA BONUS

**You'll also get two free mystery gifts!**
**(worth about $10)**

# FREE!

**Return this card today to get
2 FREE BOOKS and 2 FREE GIFTS!**

**H**HARLEQUIN®

*Romance*

**YES!** Please send me 2 FREE *Harlequin® Romance* novels,
and 2 FREE mystery gifts as well. I understand I am
under no obligation to purchase anything,
as explained on the back of this insert.

❏ I prefer the regular-print edition          ❏ I prefer the larger-print edition
116/316 HDL FNMU                                    186/386 HDL FNMU

*Please Print*

| | |
|---|---|
| FIRST NAME | LAST NAME |

ADDRESS

| | |
|---|---|
| APT.# | CITY |

| | |
|---|---|
| STATE/PROV. | ZIP/POSTAL CODE |

Visit us at:
www.ReaderService.com

HR-2F-12/12

ready to disclose. She would have to lure it from him, even against his will.

At the vineyard he immediately immersed himself in work. His manner was kind, gentle, considerate, but he came to her room only for a few moments to say good-night. He would kiss her cheek when other people were there, but never when they were alone. Nor did he ever take her in his arms. He was a perfectly behaved gentle-man, but not a lover.

She guessed that he kept his distance because he was determined not to be tempted again. But it hurt that he could resist so successfully. Within herself temptation raged. At night she would listen for the moment when he put his head around the door, longing for him to come right in, sit on the bed, talk to her, give her the chance to reach out to him. But he would smile and be gone. Recalling what she'd seen in his arms at her moment of triumph she even wondered if she'd imagined it.

*No, I didn't imagine it,* she told herself fiercely. *I won't believe that.*

Lying in the darkness, she would wonder about the fu-ture, and the many different ways it could turn out. Was Lucio restrained only because he dreaded to hurt her? Or was there another reason? Was he avoiding her emo-tionally? When he'd said that meeting her was a stroke of luck, had he only been talking about business?

Once he'd said she was wonderful.

Would he ever say it again?

# CHAPTER SEVEN

Two days later Lucio set off to visit one of his other vineyards, accompanied by Charlotte. The place was fifty
miles south, in Umbria, and she looked forward to visiting an area of Italy she hadn't seen before.

She found the trip interesting rather than enjoyable. As
Lucio had warned, he would be working morning, noon
and night, and there was no time for pleasure. She accompanied him whenever possible, learned all she could
about the different varieties of grapes and listened to end-
less work discussions.

The trip was valuable for the insight it gave her into
him. Before her eyes he turned into someone else. She'd
known him first as an elegant man-about-town, then a
skilful and imaginative lover, and then an efficient man-
ager. Now that final aspect was growing harder, sharper,
revealing a man who lived for nothing but business and
shrewd, sometimes harsh dealing. For this he had the admiration of his tenants who ran the place, but not their
affection. Nor did he apparently want it.

She remembered the night they'd spent in Enrico's
palace, when he'd remarked how many different aspects
there were to her personality.

'You've already shown me several different faces,'

he'd said, 'and I'm curious to know what surprises you still have in store for me.'

She was beginning to understand what he meant. Her view of him was exactly the same.

As they drove home he asked, 'What did you think?'

Receiving no answer he glanced at her briefly and saw that she was asleep. He nodded. He didn't blame her.

He had two more visits coming up, but she gently declined the chance to go with him. He didn't protest and she had the feeling he was glad of her decision.

At home she concentrated on learning about life there, and fitting in with it. Fiorella took her to meet the neighbours, most of whom were kindly and pleasant. One family surveyed her with suppressed hostility, which Fiorella explained thus.

'Those two daughters had set their sights on Lucio, and they're furious that you've snatched him from under their noses. Good for you. I prefer you to them any day.'

Three times Lucio called her, asking how she was, assuring her that he was thinking of her. But there were always distractions in the background that caused the call to end soon.

When he returned to the Vigneto Constanza he embraced Charlotte, then stood back with his hands on her shoulders and regarded her closely. 'How are you?'

'Doing fine,' she told him.

'That's good because I've brought a couple of guests home with me. We've got a lot of business to do, but they're anxious to meet you.'

The guests took up his attention through the meal and the rest of the evening, but as she was going to bed he came into her room and opened his arms to her. She threw herself in gladly, and felt him enclose her in a fierce hug. Her heart leapt.

'How are you? Are you really all right?'

'Ready for anything,' she said, hoping he would detect her real meaning.

But he only said, 'That's the best news I've had. I drove Fiorella crazy every night demanding to know how you were. But you look fine. Come here.'

He enfolded her in another hug. She held her breath, waiting for the sweet feel of his hands drifting over her, but they never moved until he said, 'Go to bed now. Sleep well.'

He put her to bed, pulled the covers up over her and departed.

She was left staring at the ceiling, coming to terms with the discovery that while he'd called her only three times, he'd checked on her by calling Fiorella every night.

For the next few days he was preoccupied with his guests, and she decided to spend some time looking around the area, especially Florence. Lucio arranged for Aldo, one of the workers to drive her there and wait for her. But when they reached the town she sent Aldo home. He looked uneasy and she guessed Lucio had told him to stay with her if possible.

'Tell your boss I'm all right,' she said, adding firmly, 'Goodbye.'

She had an enjoyable day in Florence. When it was time to get a taxi home she paused, considered, then made her way back to the hotel where she'd stayed when she first arrived here, and where she had hired a car. As she had hoped they willingly hired her another one.

This was better, she thought as she drove back to the estate. She was happy with the welcome she'd received from the family, but she also felt a little swallowed up by it. Now she would have some freedom and independence.

She had to admit that driving across the estate was a

little confusing. The roads were unlit and twice she lost her way. But at last she saw the house, high on the hill, gleaming with lights in the darkness, and heaved a sigh of relief.

As she drew closer she saw Lucio standing there, watching her until she halted, when he strode over and opened her door.

'Where have you been?' he demanded.

'What's the problem? I've spent the past few months finding my own way around Italy and I can manage these few miles. And I called to say I'd be late.'

'Yes, Fiorella told me, but I didn't expect you to be as late as this. Can't you understand that I—?'

He stopped, clearly searching for words and not finding them. The next moment he reached for her and pulled her fiercely against him, holding her in a grip of iron. His breath was hot against her cheek.

'Hours and hours and you didn't come home,' he growled. 'Anything could have happened to you.'

He drew back a little to look at her, and she was shocked at the torment she saw in his face.

'I'm here now,' she whispered. 'It's all right. Lucio, it's all right. *It's all right.*'

'Yes…yes—'

His mouth was fierce on hers, kissing her again and again while his arms grew even tighter.

'Let me breathe,' she gasped, laughing and delighted.

'You think it's funny to put me through the wringer?'

'No, I don't think it's funny. I'm sorry, Lucio, I never imagined you'd be like this.'

'Didn't imagine I'd want to protect you? Don't you understand that I—? I don't know…I can't explain…I can't—'

She was overwhelmed by a feeling of protectiveness.

At first she'd thought he was angry, but he was distraught. Gently she took his face in her hands and kissed him.

'It's all right,' she repeated. 'And it's going to stay all right, I promise.'

'But you're not going to drive that old banger,' he said, indicating the hired car.

'Hey, you're not telling me what I can do, are you?'

'No, I'm telling you that I'm going to buy you a decent car. Think you can put up with that?'

'I guess I'll try.'

'I'm sorry, I didn't mean to upset you.'

'And I didn't mean to upset *you*.'

'When you didn't come back… These dark, unfamiliar roads—you could have had an accident. You could have—both of you.'

She nodded, touching her stomach. 'Yes, there are two of us, aren't there? I guess I wasn't thinking straight. I like my freedom, but I should have remembered that when you're pregnant you lose a lot of freedom.' She gave a rueful sigh. 'It's not just me any more. I did get lost, just for a little while.'

'Only because the roads are unfamiliar. When you've driven in and out of Florence a few times you'll know the way and have no more problems. Now come inside and have something to eat. You must be famished.'

He kept his word about the car, escorting her to the showroom next day, watching her reactions to vehicle after vehicle, until he saw her face light up with pleasure.

'That one?' he said.

'That one. Oh, no, look at the price!'

'Let me worry about that.'

The test drive confirmed her best hopes, and within an hour she was the owner.

'Now you can drive me home,' he said.

'But what about the car we came in?'

'Aldo can pick it up. Come on. This time I'm going to be the passenger.'

He did everything in his power to make her forget his agitation of the night before, and all seemed well.

But when she thought how distraught he'd been she knew there was something there that she didn't understand, something that suggested another, deeply mysterious man, tormented and troubled to the point of agony, lurking below the surface.

Who was he? How often did he emerge? And why?

Now her life was contented, even happy. Not only was Fiorella friendly but Elizabetta and all the servants combined to spoil her. They knew about the coming child, were delighted by it and would do anything to make sure she enjoyed living with them.

The only disturbances were tiny things, impossible to predict, such as the time she opened a cupboard door and found a picture of a young girl.

She knew at once that this must be Maria, and gazed, fascinated. Maria had been not merely pretty but glorious, vibrant with youth, seeming to sum up in one delicate person everything that would make life worth living.

She then saw Lucio in the photo, clasping Maria's waist and standing behind her. She couldn't see much of his face, but she could just make out that he was smiling ecstatically, and his attitude was one of triumph, the victor holding the trophy.

She put the picture carefully back and closed the door, guessing that it had been hidden away so that she should not see it. Doubtless it was kindly meant, but she couldn't help thinking that it had the perverse effect of warning her that Maria was still her rival for Lucio's heart: a rival who had no intention of giving up easily.

She lowered her head, her eyes closed, a prey to a sudden feeling of weariness, almost despair. Once again she was on the outside looking in. Her family, Don. They had all made her feel excluded. But recently things had changed. Here in Tuscany, at the vineyard, with Lucio, she had been made welcome. Or so she'd thought.

But the welcome was not complete. Suddenly the door was barred against her again, and the one who stood there, warning her that she would never get past the barrier into Lucio's heart, was Maria.

But she would refuse to yield to the treacherous feelings. Giving in was for weaklings. She was ready for the fight. If only Lucio was here, so that battle could commence.

One evening she came home to find he had arrived a day early. He greeted her cheerfully with a kiss on her cheek.

'Been exploring again?'

'Yes, but mostly the towns, which isn't what I want.'

'Surely towns are interesting. All those delightful fashion shops—'

'Yes, I've visited a few. And the shop that's going to be your wine store. But I haven't seen much of the place that interests me most.'

'And where would that be?'

'It's called the Vigneto Constanza,' she said, her head on one side as she reminded him of his own estate. 'You must have heard of it.'

He scratched his head. 'It seems vaguely familiar.'

'Everyone says it's the biggest and the best. I'd really like to explore it properly.'

He grinned. 'Then I guess I'll have to oblige.'

It was little more than a month since she'd come here to find him, but already she could see a new lushness in the grapes that would one day be Chianti wine. As they strolled down an alley he said, 'Do you remember this place?'

'Yes, this was where I told you I was pregnant. You were standing down there.'

'Watching you walk towards me from a great distance. I knew even then that you were going to cause an earthquake, but I had no idea how big it was going to be.'

'Neither had I. I knew I was pregnant but this—' She made a flourishing gesture, taking in the view for miles. 'This makes everything different.'

'Do you like it here?'

'Oh, yes, it's lovely. I've been learning as much as I can. I go online, and read books. I know that you'll harvest these grapes in October, and store them for two years before they can be wine. But that's just facts. Standing here amid all this beauty is different. But I suppose you see it more practically.'

'You think I can see only the money, but I can feel the beauty, too. When I first came here I spent a night sleeping under the stars in one of these fields. It was pure magic, and next morning I went to ask for a job because I knew I never wanted to leave. I'm glad it affects you, too.'

They strolled on, both enjoying their shared warmth and contentment. But, as often happened, it died in an argument only a moment later.

'There's been something I've been meaning to tell you,' he said. 'I don't know how you're fixed financially, but I don't want you to have any worries about that. So I've opened a bank account for you. Here.' He handed her a chequebook. 'It's all set up and I'll be making regular payments.'

But instead of eagerly taking the chequebook she stepped back and shook her head.

'No, thank you. I'd rather not.'

He stared. 'What did you say?'

'I've already opened an account for myself. I'm not in need of money, my family are fortunately very wealthy and I've saved quite a bit from my job back in New York. I wouldn't have started this trip if I couldn't finance it without help.'

'But you're carrying my child. It's my job to look after you.'

'And you're doing that. You've given me a home. I don't need any more. I appreciate you thinking of me, and I'm not ungrateful, but I won't take your money, Lucio.'

'But why?' he demanded.

'Why should I? Not all women want to take a man's money. Let's take it easy. There's a lot we still don't agree about.'

'Do we have to agree about everything?'

'Not about everything, but some things matter.'

'All right. Have it your way.' He sighed and thrust the papers back into his pocket, making a wry face. 'After all, why should I object? I can spend the money you've saved me on riotous living.'

'Naturally. That's what I hope you'll do.'

'You're the most maddening woman, do you know that?'

'Of course. I work at it.'

'Why work at it? You have a natural gift for awkwardness.'

'I'm not the only one. That's one of the things we still have to negotiate, whether my awkwardness and yours can live with each other.'

'Would you like to take bets on who'll be the winner?'

'No, that would be boring.'

He grinned. 'That's one thing I'm never afraid of with you. I'll let you win this time.'

'Coward,' she jeered.

'Whatever you say. Come on, there's a lot for you still to see.'

Charlotte wondered at herself. Lucio seemed to have offered her a gesture of acceptance, the very acceptance she was eager to find. Yet was it her he sought to bind to him, or only the child?

With all her heart she longed for him to want her for herself, and until she was certain of that she would retain some independence—however perverse and awkward she might seem, not only in his eyes but in her own.

These days she was often in contact with her family in the States, not just through email but with a video link on her new laptop.

Ellie had much to tell. She had been to see their Calhoun relatives in Larkville, Texas.

'Clay had four children,' she told Charlotte. 'Two daughters, Jess and Megan, and two sons, Holt and Nate. I haven't met all of them yet but that's going to be the next thing. Every year in October Larkville has a festival. This year it's going to include a celebration of Clay Calhoun's life, to mark the first anniversary of his death. His children really want us to be there, so I'm going to stay here for it, especially now I've met Jed, and you must come, too.' Ellie had travelled to Larkville earlier in the year wanting to know the truth about her father and had fallen in love with Larkville's sheriff, Jed Jackson.

'But I can't,' Charlotte said. 'My baby's due about then. I can't take a long flight so close to the birth. Just imagine Lucio's reaction to that idea.'

'And who's Lucio to tell you what you can and can't do?'

'He's the father. That gives him some rights.'

'But he can't tell you whether you can or can't come home.'

Home, she thought. How strange that word now sounded. Wasn't Tuscany her home now?

'What about marriage?' Ellie demanded.

'We haven't talked about it, but we get on well.'

'Charlotte, shouldn't you be facing facts now? Does he actually want to marry you? I mean, if he hasn't asked you—'

'I—'

'He hasn't, has he?'

'No, but that doesn't mean—'

'Doesn't it? Look, I care about you. I know you don't believe that after the trouble recently, but it's true. I want you to be happy, and I don't think you are. You're having his child, he's moved you into his house but he won't make it final. Doesn't that tell you something?'

Charlotte couldn't speak. Conflicting thoughts and emotions stormed through her. Her feelings were greater than Lucio's, but she'd told herself a thousand times that she could cope. Now Ellie was forcing her to face something she wanted to avoid, at least for the moment.

'What about you?' Ellie pursued remorselessly. 'Do *you* want to marry *him*?'

'Don't be so old-fashioned,' Charlotte said quickly. 'People don't have to marry these days.'

'No, but if things are right between them they want to get married. That's how you know. Does he say he loves you?'

'Look—'

'I guess that means he doesn't. For pity's sake, get

yourself back here as soon as possible. He thinks he owns you but he won't commit to you. Come home, Charlotte.'

'Ellie, I've got to go. We'll talk again soon. Goodbye.'

She shut the call down and sat with her face buried in her hands, devastated. It was no use telling herself that Ellie didn't understand the situation. The words 'He thinks he owns you but he won't commit to you' rang in her ears despite her frantic attempts to shut them out.

'It's not true,' she whispered. 'He needs time. We're close, even if it's only as friends. I can build on that.'

But in her mind was another voice, saying cruelly, *'You're fooling yourself. He doesn't care for you in the way you want, and you just believe what you want to believe.'*

'But I'm not giving up yet,' she whispered.

As part of her desire to fit in with Lucio's life she asked him to show her the shop in Florence that he had bought with Enrico. It was in the luxurious Via della Vigna Nuova, which translated as the Street of the New Vineyard. Not surprisingly it was to be a wine store.

She met Vincente, who would be in charge, organising the shop, stocking it, arranging the grand opening. She found him pleasant and receptive to the ideas that were beginning to bubble in her mind. She wanted to be involved in this venture.

As they were just about to leave there was a new arrival, the last person they expected to see there.

'Franco,' Charlotte exclaimed, holding out her hands.

'I'm not selling this place back to you,' Lucio said at once.

'Don't worry, it's all yours. But I remember I left some stuff of mine in the cupboard under the stairs.'

They helped him fetch his things, and the three of them had lunch together.

Franco continued to happily talk away in Venetian with Charlotte, until at last he switched back to Italian to say, 'I suppose you'll make a bid for one of the Bantori vineyards now.'

'I've been thinking of it,' Lucio agreed, 'but why do you say "now"?'

'Because now you have Charlotte, who speaks Venetian, you'll find a lot of things easier.'

'Venetian?' Charlotte exclaimed. 'But surely you can't grow grapes in Venice, with all those canals?'

'Not actually in Venice,' Lucio told her. 'But there are vineyards in the surrounding countryside, and I've been thinking of expanding.'

'I can put you in touch with several useful people,' Franco said.

Charlotte grew very still. An idea was creeping up on her, mischievous, delightful, a bit naughty but all the more fun for that.

Assuming a tone of serious consideration she said, 'I think we should go to Venice as soon as possible. There's important business to be done. The next few days would be a good idea.'

Lucio eyed her curiously. 'What are you up to?'

'Me?' she asked, eyes wide and innocent. 'I'm just trying to help you make money. Why would you suspect me of an ulterior motive?'

'Because I'm beginning to know you, and an ulterior motive is the first thing that comes into my head.' He grinned. 'Come on. Own up. What am I being tricked into?'

Franco began to laugh. 'Of course, I should have thought of it. Where was my head?' He beamed at Charlotte. 'I should have known that someone as knowledgeable about Italy as you would have been alert to this.'

'It's something I've always wanted to see,' she said. 'And here's my chance.'

'When you two jokers have finished,' Lucio said ironically. 'Are you going to let me in on the secret?'

'Perhaps we ought to tell him,' Franco asked.

'I reckon we'd better,' she said solemnly. Her eyes met Lucio's, his wary, hers brimming with fun.

'If we go now we'll be in time for the festival. You know—the Festa della Sensa. You must have heard of it.'

'Of course I—is it now? Yes—' He slapped his forehead.

'And you're an Italian,' Charlotte mocked.

'I'm Tuscan not Venetian. I don't keep all their festivals in my head. But I've heard of this one and I agree it would be good to go.'

The Festa della Sensa was a glorious Venetian water pageant, whose peak was the moment when a ring was tossed into the water, symbolising Venice's marriage to the sea. By sheer lucky chance it was due to start in a few days, and they would have time to get there and join in.

'You're a conniving little so-and-so,' he said when they returned to the car.

'Nonsense. I'm doing my bit as your Venetian assistant. Just wait and see how useful I can be.'

'I think I'm going to enjoy this,' he said.

'I hope so. I know I am.'

That night, somewhere in her dreams, Charlotte heard Lucio's softly murmured, 'You're wonderful.' Then she awoke and lay awake listening, longing to hear again the whisper that would bring her to life.

He'd said it to her after their night of passion. Surely one day he would say it again.

Waiting—waiting…

Light was coming in around the gaps at the blinds, and she rose to go to the window, wanting to watch the dawn. Now she felt as though light was dawning in her life. Everything in her yearned towards the trip to Venice that she would take with Lucio, share work with him, and perhaps share even more.

Then she saw something that made her grow still. At a little distance on a hill there was a man, completely still, watching the dawn. As the light slowly engulfed him she could see that it was Lucio.

What had made him go out to that isolated place to stand against the sky, so alone that he might have been the only person alive in the world?

And she remembered what he'd said about a desert that very first night; that it could be a place of safety because there was nobody to hurt you. And he'd meant exactly that. She knew it now.

With all her heart she longed to go to him, open her arms and draw him against her heart, telling him that he didn't need to live in a desert. But at this moment he would turn away from her, because the desert was what he had chosen.

She stood watching him for a long time, hoping to see him move, to return home to her. But he stood there, imprisoned in a terrible, isolated stillness.

At last she returned to bed and lay down in her own desert.

# CHAPTER EIGHT

THEY nearly didn't make the trip to Venice. With only two days to the festival every hotel for miles was booked. But a sudden cancellation came just in time.

'We're going to stay in the Tirani Hotel,' Lucio told her.

Charlotte's eyes widened. 'Wow!'

The Tirani was one of the most luxurious hotels in Venice. On her last visit she had stayed in a far more modest establishment, occasionally walking past the Tirani, just close enough to see that it was way out of her price range.

'I hope it lives up to your expectations,' Lucio said, grinning and correctly interpreting her amazement.

They travelled by train, boarding at Florence Station for the two-hour journey.

'I loved Venice when I was there before,' she said as they neared the magical city. 'But it was winter and everywhere was under snow, even the gondolas. I've always wanted to go back and see it in the sun.'

'And you managed it, by manipulating me like a puppet. Well done.'

'Oh, that's how you feel. Well, if the vineyards in the Veneto aren't worth fighting for, why don't we just go back?'

He eyed her with grimly humorous appreciation.

'If you think I'll fall for that, forget it. I know you well enough by now to reckon that you'll have researched the subject and know exactly how good they are.'

'Right! I did just that, and I know that the Bantori vineyards are well known for their white grapes, which are used to make the very best prosecco wine. In Tuscany you grow Sangiovese grapes to make red wine, so you'd probably enjoy branching out into a different area.'

'You really have been doing research,' he observed.

He wished he could have kept the touch of admiration out of his voice. It galled him to discover that he respected her brains, but he couldn't help it.

He'd never sought the company of intellectual women. Nor was that how she'd appeared on the first evening. True, she'd argued like someone whose brain was up to every trick, but soon other aspects of her had risen to distract him. Now he was discovering that to keep one step ahead of her he would need all his wits.

As she gazed out of the window he took the chance to study her, knowing that her combination of beauty and brains was likely to cause him even more trouble in the future than it had already. Pregnancy suited her, causing a glorious flowering. Yet the alertness was always there in her eyes, warning him to take nothing for granted.

He marvelled at the situation in which he found himself. He, not she, was Italian, yet in thirty-two years he had never visited Venice. But she knew the city well and was revealing it to him. Something in the irony of that appealed to his sense of humour.

Not that there had been much humour in his life. Once, briefly, he'd enjoyed a time of vibrant emotion, but when it was snatched from him he'd determined to banish feelings, clinging only to things that could be relied on. Work, money, philanthropy. He was known for his fine actions benefiting his neighbours, raising money for good causes and donating generously. Few could have guessed that this was actually another way of keeping people away. When they praised his noble generosity they did it at a distance, so there was little need to reach out to them.

Eventually he supposed a wife and child might have formed part of his schedule. To have them imposed on him out of the blue had been a shock, but one he had decided to accommodate. It was good to have an heir, and a woman who understood the kind of man he was had seemed ideal. Understanding her in return hadn't entered into his calculations. At least, not at first.

But being with her was like living with one of those legendary beings whose touch changed the world. There was no choice but to follow. Gradually he was getting into her mind, but her ability to catch him off guard was disconcerting. Sometimes even pleasant.

She turned and met his gaze.

'Nearly there,' she said, smiling.

They had reached Venice Mestre, the last railway station on the mainland before the Liberty Bridge, which stretched nearly two miles out across the lagoon to the Santa Lucia Station in Venice itself. As they crossed the water Charlotte gazed, riveted, at the view she had longed to see again ever since she had left the city.

When they got down from the train she almost ran out of the station to where it opened onto the Grand Canal, and stood, breathless with delight at the sight of the boats and the water.

'This was it,' she breathed. 'This was it! Oh, isn't it beautiful?'

Now Lucio found that she could wrong-foot him again. Charlotte the efficient researcher had vanished, replaced by Charlotte the eager child, ready to plunge into a delicious fantasy.

'This is where I have to rely on you,' he said. 'What do we do now?'

In a city where the roads were made of water there was no place for wheeled vehicles. To get to the hotel they must either walk through the multitude of little back alleys, or travel by motorboat.

'We could get onto a *vaporetto*,' she said, indicating a huge water bus that had just docked. 'But a taxi's better. Over there.'

She pointed to where a group of motorboats were moored, ready for passengers. In a moment they were aboard, gliding along the Grand Canal, between the palaces, beneath the great bridges, until they reached the hotel. The receptionist greeted Lucio with the awe due to a man who'd hired the most expensive suite.

The place lived up to all Charlotte's expectations. She had her own bedroom, next to Lucio's, with a view of the canal. Looking out she saw Lucio at his own window, just a few feet away. He nodded.

'I'm glad we came.'

*'Hey!'*

A cry from below made them look down to see Franco standing up in a boat, hailing them.

'You're here!' he yelled. 'That's wonderful! Tonight you will be my guests for dinner. I have important people for you to meet. I'll collect you in an hour.'

Charlotte sighed as she saw her dream of dinner alone with Lucio vanish. But there was no choice. Doubtless the 'important people' Franco mentioned would have something to do with vineyards. This trip was about business, and she mustn't let herself forget that.

While she was unpacking her cell phone rang. It was Ellie.

'Is he there with you?' she wanted to know.

'Not in the room, but we're in Venice together.'

'Has he mentioned any further commitment?'

'No, but—'

'Charlotte, you've done some pretty mad things in your time, but this is something that affects us all. We think you should come home. You can't cope alone.'

'I'm not alone. I'm living with nice people who are kind to me.'

'But you can't mean to stay there for good. You belong here, with your family.'

'Family? Belong? Ellie, do you know how hollow those words sound to me now?'

She heard her voice sounding sharper than she'd intended and checked herself.

'I can't talk now. I have to go out—'

'Can't it wait? This is important.'

'And my life here is important to me.'

'If we could just talk about—'

Suddenly Charlotte felt her temper rising.

'No. Not now. When I'm ready to talk I'll call you. Goodbye, I've got to go now.'

She hung up, wishing Ellie hadn't chosen this moment to make contact. The last thing she wanted to think about was her old life, not when her new one was so tempting.

For the evening she chose her attire with great care. Something suitable for a business meeting, yet which would attract Lucio. At last she chose a cocktail dress of black velvet. It would be the last time she could fit into it for a while, and she was going to make the best of what it could do for her. Lucio was determined to behave 'properly' as he saw it, making no sexual claims on her for fear of causing harm. But she knew there was no need to fear harm, and while she still had the chance she was going to get him to behave 'improperly,' no matter what it took.

She knew she was on the right track when she saw his face, eyes alight with admiration, a smile that he was trying to keep under control, and not entirely succeeding.

'Do I look like an efficient assistant?' she asked. 'All ready to do my duty?'

'Is that how you're trying to look?'

'Well, this is going to be a working meal, isn't it?'

'Is it?' He sounded baffled.

'Who do you think these "important people" are that Franco wants us to meet? They must be something to do with the vineyards. Obviously they're friends of his and he's helping them find a buyer. That's why he suggested you might want to buy a Veneto vineyard, and why he's bringing you together.' She met his gaze with well-contrived innocence. 'Surely that's obvious?'

'Yes—yes, of course,' he said hastily. He pulled himself together. 'I can see you're going to be an excellent assistant. I'm impressed.'

Franco was waiting downstairs, ready to lead them the short distance to the restaurant.

'There will be ten of us,' he said. 'My son has recently become engaged, and will be joining us with his fiancée, Ginevra. Also Ginevra's parents will be there. You'll have a lot in common with them, Lucio. They own several vineyards around here.'

Charlotte stole a sly glance at Lucio and found him looking right back at her. As their eyes met each knew the other was suppressing a smile.

'I think you must be psychic,' he whispered in her ear.

'You might find that a very useful gift in an assistant.'

'An assistant isn't exactly what I had in mind. Yes, Franco, we're just coming.'

Together they walked on, each wondering exactly what the other was thinking, and each thoroughly enjoying it.

In the restaurant they found the four people Franco had described, also his wife, who greeted them with a beaming smile. Charlotte found herself sitting next to Rico, owner of the vineyard, with Lucio on his other side, confirming her suspicions that this was a work meeting.

She did what was expected of her, speaking Venetian, making the occasional error and leading the laughter at her own expense. As the evening moved on the mood became increasingly friendly. Rico, in particular, was happy to talk to Charlotte. The subject was his vineyard but he seemed unable to take his eyes off her, as Lucio in particular noticed.

There was a brief, awkward moment when her cell phone rang and she answered it to find Alex.

'I've been talking to Ellie,' she said. 'She's worried about you, and we were both think—'

'I can't talk now,' she said hastily. 'I'll call back. Bye.'

She shut the phone down and switched it off, cursing herself for not doing so before. Everyone was looking at her with interest, as though speculating who her caller might be.

She turned her brightest smile on Rico. 'I really look forward to seeing your estate,' she said.

'And I hope you will come very soon, perhaps tomorrow,' he declared fervently.

'That would be excellent,' Lucio said before she could reply. 'May I suggest an early start?'

They all agreed on an early start.

'Then I think we won't stay out too late tonight,' Lucio

said. 'An early start tomorrow means an early night now. Are you ready, my dear?'

'Quite ready,' she said.

'Oh, surely, just a little longer—' Franco protested.

'I look forward to tomorrow,' Lucio interrupted him.

As they strolled back to the hotel she said, 'Were you wise to risk offending him? After all, if you're going to do business—'

'I'm the buyer. I make the terms. And if he rakes you with his eyes like that again I'll—I don't know…'

'Knock a few thousand off the price you offer?' she suggested.

'I had something else in mind,' he growled.

'Nonsense! Money's far more effective. He badly needs to sell that vineyard.'

'He told you that?'

'Not in so many words, but it came through. He's had a lot of "expenses" recently, by which I think he means gambling debts. His wife said the word *casino* in a certain tone that spoke volumes. They're planning a lavish wedding for their daughter and counting on the money from the vineyard. So you've got the advantage.'

'I'd still rather punch his lights out.'

'Only the money matters. Cling to that.'

'Yes, ma'am! You're really getting the hang of this.'

'Right. I think I missed my vocation. I should have gone into big business. Since I've been here I've seen a whole new future opening up, chief of a money-making enterprise, giving orders left, right and centre—' She stopped, glancing up at his face. 'All right, I'm only joking.'

'And I fall for it so easily, don't I?'

'You have your moments.'

'Fine, go ahead. Have fun. My time will come.'

*My time will come.* She'd said this to herself so often that hearing it from Lucio caught her by surprise. Suddenly she glimpsed thoughts and feelings inside him that she had never suspected. Was he really holding his breath for what could happen between them? Just like herself?

'I suppose I shouldn't have dragged you away like that,' he mused.

'No, you shouldn't. I was still eating a lovely cake.'

'Then I'll buy you another one.'

'First you bought me a car, now a cake,' she teased. 'What next? You think money buys you out of any situation, don't you?'

'Of course it does. You just taught me that, and I'm learning. Let's go in there.'

He indicated a little café just up ahead, and soon they were sitting at a table, being served with cake and sparkling water.

'You can drink alcohol if you want,' Charlotte said. 'Are you afraid that I'll be tempted if I see a bottle of wine? No need. I'm quite grown up. Honestly.'

He made a face and ordered some wine. 'I was trying to be considerate.'

'Thank you for the thought but there's no need.' She gave a blissful sigh. 'Oh, I did enjoy today.'

'I'm glad to see you in a happier mood.'

'Whatever do you mean? I haven't been grumpy, have I?'

'Not with me, but whoever you were talking to on the phone earlier today. I heard you from the next room. You sounded ready to bite their head off.'

'Oh, that! Yes, I wasn't at my best.'

'This person did something to annoy you?'

She made a wry face. 'You could say she's been annoying me since the day we met, twenty-seven years ago.'

'Family?'

'Sister. Well, half-sister. I've always been fond of her but I can't help resenting her, too. She's so beautiful, so elegant. Men have always pursued her and she has to fend them off. Honestly, sometimes I could have murdered her for being so gorgeous.'

'Don't underestimate your own looks.'

'Oh, come on!' She turned to regard herself in the wall mirror, giving a disparaging flick to her long hair. 'I'm not beautiful.'

'You're striking,' he said, recalling how her hair had looked spread out over the pillow. 'I have no complaints.'

'That's because you're a gentleman with perfect manners.'

'Liar!' He grinned. 'Well, I had to say something. Was that her who called you during the meal?'

'No, that was my other sister Alex.'

'Is she gorgeous, too?'

'She's pretty, but she has something more important than looks. She has charm. And don't you dare tell me I'm charming.'

'I swear it never crossed my mind. I'm much too afraid of you.'

'Good. Keep it that way.'

'So how did Ellie offend you?'

'Nothing special,' she said quickly. 'She was just concerned about how I was managing.'

'But you sounded annoyed.'

'Yes, well—they have their own ideas but it doesn't concern them, and I don't want them interfering.'

'Is this what you hinted at the first night? You mentioned an older brother and sister who were twins and a younger sister. But you said there was a big family secret, and you were the last to know. It made you feel like an outsider.'

'Yes.' She sighed. 'My father is my mother's second husband. Before him she was married to a man called Clay Calhoun, but the marriage broke up, she left him and met Cedric Patterson soon after. They planned to marry, then she discovered that she was pregnant by Clay. But Cedric still wanted her. They married and she had twins, Ellie and Matt, which my father raised as his own.

'But recently we found out that my mother wrote to Clay telling him about her pregnancy. If he'd responded she might never have married my dad. But he didn't because he never got the letter. Sandra, the new woman in his life, kept it from him and then they got married.

'She died a couple of years ago, and Clay died last year. His daughter Jess was going through his things when she found a box belonging to Sandra, and the letter was in it. That's how she learned that her father had two other children.

'I think she had to search for them on the internet. At last she found Ellie and told her. So just a few months ago she and Matt discovered that they were Clay's children, and not our father's. She told Alex first, I guess because she's always been closer to her, but she delayed telling me.'

'Hell!' Lucio exclaimed.

'Yes, that's how I felt. You remember the hotel in Rome where we met?'

'The Hotel Geranno.'

'Right. I'd just been down to their internet café and found an email from Alex telling me all about it. From Alex, not from Ellie. She couldn't even be bothered to email me herself, not about that nor the fact that she seems to have found "Mr Right". I felt I'd come at the end of a long queue.'

Lucio took her hand and squeezed it. 'They shouldn't have done that to you.'

'I felt so unwanted, unnecessary, surplus to requirements, don't call us, we'll call you—or perhaps not.' She sighed. 'Until then I'd always felt so pleased about having a family—a "real family" as I called it. With a family you weren't alone. Only then I discovered I was wrong.'

'But Ellie and Matt are still your siblings even if you do only share one parent now. And Alex is your full sister.'

'Yes.' She sighed.

'But that doesn't help much, does it? Is there no one in the family who could help you? Your parents?'

'I can't talk to them about this. A while back my father's mind started to go. These days he's very confused and looking after him is my mother's priority. Nothing else really matters to her, so when I called her—'

'She wouldn't talk to you about it?' he asked, frowning.

'Not exactly. She confirmed it had happened, but she said it was all a long time ago, and why should I worry about it? Obviously it involves Matt and Ellie because they're Clay's children, but I'm not, and she didn't seem to think it concerned me.'

'But a family upheaval like that concerns everyone.'

'That's how I think, but my mother doesn't seem to understand. I used to feel close to her—well, sort of. The twins were special and Alex is gorgeous. I'm the middle one and I don't stand out like the others. I've always felt that, and sometimes I've acted a bit daft, trying to attract attention, I suppose. Some of them call me the rebel of the family, some call me the idiot—'

'Stop right there,' he interrupted her. 'You're going to put yourself down and I won't have it.'

She smiled. 'Well, I can't help remembering what that man at the party said about women who—'

'*That's enough!* He knows nothing.' Lucio laid his hand over hers. 'At least, he doesn't know what I know.'

'Thank you,' she choked.

'You'll sort it with your family one day.'

'Will I? I don't know. They've made me feel so shut out. You know that saying, "Home is the place where they have to let you in". Now it's as though they wouldn't let me in.'

'That feeling won't last. You need time to get over it, but it'll happen. After all, you have another home now.'

She studied him curiously, aware of the mysterious sensation that had overcome her before in his company, as though their minds were in harmony. Even Matt, the sibling to whom she'd always felt close, hadn't given her such a feeling.

Had he ever? she mused. His failure to tell her what the others knew had left her feeling distant from him. But even in the past, had she felt as she did now with Lucio, that she'd found a friend to confide in? In time he might be more, but best friend was the least she would settle for.

'Is something funny?' he asked, watching her.

'I was just thinking what a wonderful brother you'd make, which I suppose is a bit funny in the circumstances.'

'Not really. You and I need to be friends, allies, comrades.'

'That's true. We always could read each other's minds, couldn't we?'

'From the first moment,' he agreed. 'Remember that argument we had at that café near the Trevi Fountain? I kept having a weird sensation that I knew exactly what you were going to say next. And you usually did.'

'That must have made me very boring,' she said lightly.

He shook his head. 'No, you're never boring. Don't put yourself down. You were in a bad way that night, and you needed someone. I'm glad it was me.'

He raised her hand and laid his cheek against the back.

'So that's why I got lucky,' he said softly. 'I've always wondered.'

'What do you mean?'

'Well, I could tell that you're not the kind of girl who goes in for one-night stands. Even if you are the rebel of the family, it was the first time your rebellion had ever taken that particular form, wasn't it?'

She nodded.

'But it happened with me. I'm not conceited enough to think you fell for my "looks and charm". You felt sad and lonely and I just happened to be there.'

'It was a bit more than that,' she said huskily. 'You made me feel wanted.'

'I'm glad. And you know what I'm even more glad about? That it was me and nobody else. You were so vulnerable. You could have been hurt.'

'But not by you,' she said, smiling.

'No, not by me. You made me feel wanted, too, and I guess it filled a need, just at the right time. It's almost enough to make you believe in fate. You needed me, I needed you, fate brought us together.'

'You didn't need me,' she said. 'Don't forget I saw you in the hotel, surrounded by admirers. Or do I mean worshipers? There wasn't a woman there who wouldn't gladly have changed places with me.'

'And did you see me inviting them?'

'You wouldn't have had to try very hard,' she said wryly.

'If you mean that I lived a self-indulgent life in those days, I don't deny it.' He pulled a self-mocking face. 'But that's over. I haven't slept with another woman since I found you.'

'You mean since the day I told you about the baby?'

'No, I mean since that night in Rome. Yes, I don't blame you for looking cynical, but it's true.'

'But why should you? I mean, you didn't expect ever to see me again.'

'I know. But somehow you were still with me. There were times I was tempted but you always stepped in and made me back off. I found myself living like a monk.'

He saw her gazing at him in astonishment. 'It's the truth, I swear it. Say you believe me. But only if you mean it.'

For a moment she was lost for words. This was the last thing she'd expected to hear.

He made a wry face, misunderstanding her silence.

'I guess I can't blame you. I probably wouldn't believe me either.'

'But I do,' she murmured. 'I do believe you.'

Incredibly, she really did.

'Do you really mean that?' he persisted. 'Truly?'

'Truly.'

'Thank you. Not many people would, given the way I've lived, dashing around, enjoying a superficial life. But once there was you, something changed.'

'But suppose you hadn't made me pregnant, and I hadn't come to find you?'

'That doesn't bear thinking about.'

She knew a surge of pleasure so intense that she struggled to hide it. She managed by retreating into cynicism.

'Oh, come on!' she jeered lightly. 'If it hadn't been me it would have been one of those willing ladies.'

'Most of those "willing ladies" have husbands or make a career out of being available. And they're all the kind of people that I can't get close to—not as we've grown close. I can talk to you like nobody else. I'm close to Fiorella but there are things I can't confide in her about. She's been hurt too much, I have to protect her.'

'And that's my big advantage?' she teased. 'I don't need protection.'

'Hey! You've missed no opportunity to tell me that you can look after yourself. I've lost count of the number of times you've said it as a way of slapping me down.'

'Some men need slapping down, preferably as often as possible.'

'Duly noted.' He gave a mock salute.

'But I guess in future I'll have to find another way.'

'I'm sure you'll think of something.' He grasped her hand and gave it a squeeze. 'But seriously, of course you need my protection. As though I'd let you of all people run any risks. But I do know that you're strong and independent. If it came to a battle between us I'd back you against me.'

'So would I. Let's agree on that.'

'I guess we should be going,' he said. 'It's late and you should be in bed.'

'I'm not a child to be sent to bed.'

'I'm making sure you're all right. Isn't that what I'm supposed to do?'

'Just be careful not to push your luck.'

'Let's go.'

Together they strolled out. The street was narrow, and above it was a fine strip of sky, glittering with stars. Charlotte gazed up entranced.

'It's as though they're pointing the way home,' she said. 'Just a few yards and then— Whoops!'

'Careful!' he said, grasping her as she stumbled, nearly losing her balance. 'If you don't look where you're going I guess you do need someone to keep an eye on you, after all.'

'Well, perhaps you're right.'

His arm was now firmly around her shoulders, and it was natural to lean her head back against it.

'You're still not looking at the road,' he reproved her.

'With you to guide me I don't need to. I leave everything in your hands.'

'Hm! Why does that submissive act fill me with suspicion?'

'I can't think.'

She slipped her arm about his waist and, like this, laughing and holding on to each other, they drifted on their way.

# CHAPTER NINE

Early next morning a motorboat collected them from the hotel and drove them to Piazzale Roma, the car park on the edge of town, beyond which no wheeled vehicle was allowed. Here they all loaded into Franco's palatial car to be driven over the Liberty Bridge onto the mainland, and from there another fifty miles to the vineyard.

There Rico met them and gave them a conducted tour through his magnificent fields. What little Charlotte had seen of vineyards was enough to tell her that this was a splendid place, and the greatest favour she could do for Lucio was stay in the shadows.

She could tell that he was impressed by what he saw and heard, although his outward response was muted, as befitted a man with money at stake. Occasionally Rico would address her in Venetian, but only as a courtesy. Serious business was conducted in Italian, and increasingly she sensed that all was going well.

She particularly liked the house; not a palace like the ones she saw in Tuscany, but sprawling with an air of warmth and friendliness. Children could live happily here, she thought, wandering through the rooms.

At last there were handshakes and smiles all round. It was settled, and everyone was pleased.

'Tonight we meet again in Venice, to celebrate,' Rico declared. 'You will all be my guests.'

On the journey back Lucio and Franco continued an animated discussion on the necessary arrangements. Charlotte stayed quiet, but made notes.

Back in the hotel she adjusted her attire a little more than last night, choosing a neckline just an inch lower to take advantage of her generous bosom. Lucio made no comment, but the way he nodded told her something she wanted to know. She was determined to believe that.

The evening was a triumph. There were the same guests as the night before, and everyone involved in the deal felt they had gained.

'I can't thank you enough,' Lucio murmured as he clinked glasses with Charlotte.

'For what? I've kept my mouth firmly shut all day.'

'I could say that a woman who knows when to do that is worth her weight in gold, but you'd probably accuse me of being a sexist beast, so I won't. It was clever of you not to get involved in the negotiations—'

'Since they would have been over my head.'

'Will you stop trying to trap me, you little fiend? And stop laughing.'

'No, why should I?'

'I meant that you made the negotiations happen. Without you I probably wouldn't be here, and I'd have lost a lot.'

'So if it turns into a disaster it'll be all my fault?'

'Of course. What else?'

She began to laugh and he joined in. Glancing at them Franco thought that he had never seen a couple who belonged together so completely. He turned away to make a discreet call on his cell phone.

The rest of the evening was spent discussing the festival next day. At last Franco rose to his feet.

'We shall all meet again tomorrow,' he said, 'to take part in the festival. But now I have something else to say. Work is important, but this is also an evening for couples. My son and his future wife are a couple, my friends Charlotte and Lucio are a couple. My wife and I recently celebrated our wedding anniversary, and you—' he indicated Ginevra's parents '—will celebrate yours next month. So tonight I've arranged something special. Ah, I think it's here now.'

He looked up at a man, dressed as a gondolier, signalling him from the doorway.

'They are waiting for us,' he said. 'Shall we go?'

One of the doors of the restaurant opened on to a little side canal. There they found five gondolas ready to receive them.

'A romantic journey for each of us,' Franco said. 'Goodnight until tomorrow.'

Hardly believing that this was happening, Charlotte took the hand that the gondolier held out to her, and climbed in carefully. When all the boats were full the procession glided away.

Looking around Charlotte saw the other three couples snuggled happily in each other's arms. Franco was clearly a master of show business—a gondola ride in Venice, the very essence of romance.

Cheers and jeers rose from the other three boats when the occupants saw that Lucio and Charlotte were the only couple not embracing.

'Go on, spoilsport!'

'Why don't you kiss her?'

From Rico came words in Venetian which made Charlotte laugh.

'What did he say?' Lucio demanded.

'Something rather rude about you.'

'Tell me.'

'No way.'

'I see. Then I'll just have to put him right.'

He tightened his arm, laying his mouth against hers in a theatrical manner that made their companions cheer even more raucously.

Charlotte restrained her impulse to pull him closer, knowing that this was just more showmanship. If only they could be alone. Then she could do everything she wanted to turn showmanship into reality.

It was the gondolier who came to her rescue, calling in Venetian, *'Dove voi andare?'*

'What was that?' Lucio murmured.

'He asked where we want to go.'

*'Canale Grande?'* the boatman called. *'Ponte di Rialto?'*

'Do you want to see the Grand Canal and the Rialto Bridge?' she translated.

Lucio shook his head. 'I'd prefer something a little quieter, more private.'

'We'll keep to the little back canals,' she called.

*'Sì, signorina.'*

Now it was like being in another universe, created from narrow alleys, gleaming water and darkness. The boatman made no intrusive comments and they could imagine they were alone in the whole world.

'Your night of triumph,' he murmured.

'Hardly,' she said, thinking of how much she still had to achieve. 'It doesn't feel like triumph. Not yet.'

His eyes met hers, seeking her true meaning.

'What would make it a triumph?' he asked softly.

'You,' she said, reaching for him. 'Only you.'

This was her kiss. She was the prime mover, and knew that her triumph was beginning. She slipped her arms above his head, determined that this time he would not escape, but he had no thought of escape. She could tell that with every fibre of her being.

She had dreamed of this ever since he'd fled from her at Enrico's home, making love to her and then setting a cruel distance between them. Now everything she longed for was being given back to her. Every movement of his lips was a promise, and she would reclaim that promise with interest. She assured herself that while her sense of triumph soared.

A slight bump announced that the gondola had arrived at the hotel. Dazed, they wandered into the hotel and up to their suite. But there he paused, and a little fear crept over her. To conquer it she drew him close again. He put his arms about her, gentle, almost tentative.

'Charlotte, I—'

'It's all right,' she whispered against his mouth. 'Everything's all right.'

'Is it? Can you be sure? I know myself. I can't be near you without wanting to do something selfish. Just touching you brings me to the edge of control.'

'Good. That's where I want you—until you leap over the edge completely.'

'Or until you lure me over.' He tightened his arms, speaking in a tense voice. 'I've tried to be strong but you're not going to let me, are you?'

'Not for a moment.'

'Charlotte, don't—don't— *Charlotte!*'

And then there was only the feeling of victory as he drew her into his bedroom, pulling at her clothes. She would have helped him but he moved too fast for her, so she ripped his off instead.

No doubts, no hesitation, no false modesty. Just the plain fact that her will was stronger than his.

'*Charlotte...*'

'*Yes, yes...*'

His eyes, looking down on her, were mysteriously fierce and tender at the same time. 'You're a wicked woman,' he whispered.

'You'd better get used to it.'

'In a thousand years I'll never get used to you.'

He laid his head down against her breast and she wrapped him lovingly in her arms. There was still a way to go yet, but they would get there. In time she would win everything she wanted. In time he would be all hers.

After a while she felt him move, raise his head and grow still again, looking down on her.

'Are you all right?' he whispered.

'Of course I am.'

'Are you sure?' Now he was backing away, leaving the bed, until she reached out and stopped him.

'Oh, Lucio, please—don't do this again.'

'What do you mean?'

'I mean that last time we made love you ran from me as fast as you could, as though it had been a traumatic experience for you. Am I really so terrible?'

'The terrible one is me, selfishly taking what I want when you—'

'Then you're not the only selfish one, because *I* want it, too.'

He gave a sigh that was part a groan, and sat on the edge of the bed, running his hands through his hair.

'You probably think I'm mad, being so paranoid. Perhaps I am.'

'Lucio, I do understand, honestly I do. But no harm

will come to me because of what we've done. Or to our child.'

'But things happen so easily. Just when you think everything's going well it's all snatched away from you. And you start to feel it might be better to have nothing, than to have something precious and lose it.'

'Why don't you tell me everything?' she asked gently. 'I have the feeling that there's so much you're keeping from me. Can't you trust me?'

'I do trust you, but it can be so hard to— Do you remember the night we met, the life I was living then?'

'Yes, you seemed on top of the world. Everyone wanted your attention, everyone was out to attract you.'

'Huh!' He gave a bleak laugh. 'That may be how it looked but it was an empty life. I felt that all the time— bleak, meaningless—but I couldn't live any other way. There was nothing else for me in those days. I had no anchor, and I didn't want one.'

'Didn't want one? As bad as that?' she asked softly.

He nodded.

'Tell me how it happened.'

'It started so long ago that I can barely remember it— the place, the people, everything I once called home.'

'Before you came to Tuscany?'

He nodded.

Now she knew she must tread carefully. Seeking him online she had several times found him described as a man of mystery.

'He appeared from nowhere,' one article had said. 'Nobody seems to know where he came from, or, if they know, something—or someone—has persuaded them to keep silent.'

She sat in silence, refusing to ask any questions. What

happened now must be his choice. At last he began to speak.

'Sometimes I feel so far away from that world that it's almost as though it never existed. But when I'm honest with myself I know that it shaped me, created the dark side of me.'

'The dark side?'

'The part of my nature that's capable of revenge, ruthlessness—deliberate cruelty.'

She was about to protest but something held her silent. She'd never seen cruelty in Lucio, but instinct told her it was there. Driven too far he would be capable of the most terrible acts, the most coldly savage indifference.

Somewhere a warning voice whispered, *Leave him. Flee quickly while there's time. He's only using you because he wants the child and one day he'll break your heart. You know that. Don't you?*

*Yes,* she thought. *I know that. But I won't ever leave him.*

*Because I can't.*

*Because I'll never give up hope.*

*Because I love him.*

The words seemed to leap out at her. She hadn't meant to admit the truth, even to herself. But it had crept up on her without warning and now there was no escape.

He was watching her, seemingly troubled by her silence.

'Now you know the worst of me,' he said. 'Don't tell me you never suspected.'

She shook her head. 'You're wrong. I won't know the worst until I discover it for myself. And perhaps I never will. Stop trying to blacken yourself. Just tell me about this "other world". You had to escape it, but you've never really left it behind, have you?'

'No, I guess that's true.'

'The night we met you told me you came from Sicily. Did you have a large family?'

'No, just three of us, my parents and me. My father was a lawyer, but a very particular kind of lawyer, as I came to realise. His clients were rich and powerful. At first all I saw was that he was powerful, too. I admired him, wanted to be like him. I'd have done anything for his good opinion, or even just his attention.'

'He ignored you?'

'Not exactly. In his way he was a good father, did everything correctly. But I never felt that I was important to him. He only really loved one person in the world, and that was my mother. She was the same. Only he existed. They had the sort of marriage that most people would say was charming and idyllic.'

'Not if you were the child looking in from the outside,' she said.

For a moment he didn't react. Then, very slowly, he smiled and nodded.

'Yes,' he said. 'Of course you understand. I suppose I knew you would.'

'If your parents really love each other, you're never going to come first with either of them.'

'That's true, although to be fair to them they were kind and affectionate, in their way. As long as things went well. It was just when it came to a crisis—' He stopped.

'And one day the crisis came?' she asked softly.

He nodded. 'My father wanted me to become a lawyer. When I'd finished my training he reckoned I could become his partner. He gave me a job fetching and carrying in his office, so that I could "get the feel". That's when I started to realise what his clients were like, what he was like. He made his living protecting men who used violence and cruelty to get their way. He didn't care what they were like or what they'd done, as long as they paid him well.

'What really hurt was that he didn't understand why I minded. He called me a weakling for "making a fuss about nothing". No son of his would be such a fool. I knew I had to leave but I stayed for a while, hoping to persuade my mother to come with me. I couldn't believe she knew the truth about him, and I was sure when she learned it she'd want to flee him, as well.

'But when I told her, all she said was, "I knew you'd find out one day. I told him he should explain carefully". She kept saying my father was a good man who did what he had to for the sake of his family. But I couldn't believe it. He didn't do it for us. He did it because he wanted money at any cost, and he got a kick out of associating with crooks, as long as they were successful crooks. I begged her to come with me, but she wouldn't. She gave me some money and stood at the window as I slipped away one night.

'That was the last time I ever saw her. Three years later they were both dead. Someone killed my father and she died trying to save him. She didn't have to die, but she preferred that to living without him. Then I remembered something she'd said just before we parted, when she was trying to explain why she chose him above everything else, good and bad.'

He fell silent, and there was such pain in his face that Charlotte reached out and touched his cheek.

'Don't talk about it if you can't bear to,' she said.

'No, I want to tell you. I know I can rely on you to— to know…to feel.'

'Yes,' she whispered.

'She said that one day I'd know what it was to love someone beyond reason.'

'That's what we all hope for,' Charlotte murmured.

'Yes. She said I should be glad, for without it life would be empty. And she was right.'

'You found that out yourself?'

He squeezed her hand. From somewhere she found the resolve to say, 'You found it with Maria?'

He nodded.

'Did you fall in love with her at once?'

'No, we used to squabble a lot, but not seriously. Her parents took me in and I just seemed to fit in at once. I loved the life. I belonged. As Maria and I grew up we became closer until at the end it was just what my mother had predicted. Love beyond reason. I began to understand why she'd chosen to die rather than live without my father.'

'That must have been…earth-shattering,' she said softly. 'And beautiful.'

'Yes,' he said in a husky voice. 'Yes.'

From outside came a roar of laughter. She rose quickly and went to close the window, determined to protect Lucio. His memories were tormenting him and the last thing he needed was disturbance from outside. At all costs she would prevent that.

Before returning to him she took a moment to sort out her thoughts, which were confused. She wanted his love, and it might seem unwise to talk with him about Maria, the woman he'd loved. Yet she needed to understand how deep that love had gone, for only then could she guess her own chance of winning his heart.

She turned back to him, then paused at what she saw.

Lucio was sitting with his head sunk so low it almost reached his knees. His whole being radiated pain and despair, and she felt as though her heart would break for him.

He looked up. The sight of her brought a tense smile to his face, and he stretched out his hand in a way that was almost a plea.

'I'm here,' she said, hurrying over and clasping his hand. 'I'll always be here.'

'Will you? *Will you?*'

'Of course. I promise.'

He lifted his head and she gasped at the tragedy and desolation in his eyes.

'It's easy to promise.' He groaned. 'But nobody is always there.'

'Did she promise?' Charlotte asked softly.

'Many times. She vowed she'd never leave me—never in life—and she didn't leave me in life. She left me in death. She was so young. Her death was the one thing we never thought of.'

'How did it happen?'

'She went to Florence one afternoon, to do some shopping. I saw her driving home and waved. The next minute the car swerved, hit a rock by the roadside and overturned. I managed to get her to hospital. She was terribly hurt, there seemed to be no hope, but still I—'

He choked into silence. His eyes were closed again, as though he'd chosen to retreat back into a private world. But his fingers clutched Charlotte's hand convulsively. She laid her other hand over his, sending him comfort in the only way that could reach him.

'She lived for two days,' Lucio said softly. 'Mostly she was unconscious. Sometimes she opened her eyes and seemed to look at me, but even then I'm not sure if she could see me. I begged her not to leave me, to forgive me—'

'Forgive you? Surely she had nothing to forgive?'

'I may have caused her accident, waving when I did. Perhaps I distracted her, perhaps she waved back and took her attention off the road—'

'Lucio, don't—'

'But for me she might not have died.'

'That's just your imagination—how could you be sure?'

'I can't,' he said with soft violence. 'That's what's so terrible. I'll never know but I'll believe it all my days. I did it. *I killed her.* How can I ever have peace?'

'By asking yourself what she would have wanted,' Charlotte said. 'Maria loved you. Surely you know that, deep in your heart?'

'Yes, I—'

'If you let this idea wreck your life you're being unfair to her, to her memory. Did she manage to say anything to you before she died?'

'Yes, she said she loved me.'

'Of course she did. Her last message to you was love, so that you would always remember it. She was trying to give you peace. Don't refuse her the last thing she wanted.'

He didn't reply, and she wondered if he'd even heard her. But then he leaned towards her, resting his head on her shoulder so that his face was hidden. His clasp on her tightened, sending her a silent message, and she clasped him back.

Would she one day regret what she was doing? Instead of banishing Maria's ghost she was restoring her to him. But nothing mattered but to ease Lucio's suffering and perhaps even give him some happiness. If it meant that she herself was the loser, she would find a way to live with that.

'I'm sorry,' he said. 'I shouldn't really be talking to you about this.'

'Why not? Remember what we said? Friends, allies, comrades? I'm the best friend you have, and you can tell me anything, any time.'

'Thank you,' he said softly. 'You don't know what a comfort that is—what it's like never to be able to talk to anyone.'

'What about Fiorella?'

'I never could. Maria's death caused her such pain— how could I make it worse? And then her husband died only a year later. She's suffered such unbearable pain.'

'So you protected her,' Charlotte said.

He protected everyone, and they had all left him alone, she thought, her heart aching for him. But he wasn't alone now, and she must let him know that.

'You're exhausted,' she said. 'Lie down and go to sleep.'

Gently she pulled him down onto the bed, drawing him across her so that his head rested on her chest. A mirror in the corner gave her a slight glimpse of his face, enough to show that his eyes were closed. Everything about him radiated contentment.

'That's it,' she whispered. 'Now you can do whatever you like. We can talk if you like, because there's nothing you can't tell me, and I promise never to do anything to make you regret it. Or you can sleep in my arms. And don't worry about anything, because your friend is here.'

He stirred, and she felt the warmth of his breath against her skin. She stroked his face, laying her lips against his hair, whispering, 'She's here, and she'll always be here, as long as you need her.'

# CHAPTER TEN

SHE awoke to the sound of music from the canal below. It was the day of the glorious water parade, and the wedding to the sea, and all Venice was alive with pleasure and expectation.

'It's going to be wonderful,' she murmured, reaching for him.

He wasn't there.

In an instant she was back in the nightmare, alone, rejected, unwanted, first by her family, then by Lucio.

'No,' she groaned. 'No, *no, oh, please, no!*'

At once the door was flung open and Lucio hurried in.

'Charlotte, whatever's the matter?'

'Nothing,' she choked, 'nothing—I—'

He sat on the bed, placing his hands on her shoulders.

'Then why are you crying? Why were you calling out? What's upset you?'

'Just a nightmare,' she floundered frantically. 'I can't even remember....'

*You vanished and all my demons began shrieking again.*

But she couldn't tell him that.

'No time for nightmares,' he said merrily. 'Franco has just called to say he expects us on his boat at nine o'clock. So I've ordered breakfast up here and then we must be off.'

He kissed her cheek and retreated to the bathroom.

Left alone, she took some deep breaths, trying to focus her mind on the day ahead, but it was hard when dazzling memories still lived inside her. Last night they had achieved perfect physical union, and it had been beautiful. But just as beautiful had been the emotional and mental union that followed. He had called her his friend, and she had assured him that was what she would be.

But a friend could be a lover, too, and in time he would understand that. This was her promise to herself.

By nine o'clock a multitude of boats had gathered in the water next to St Mark's Square, and within fifteen minutes they had moved off in a colourful parade across the lagoon to the Lido island. Rowers in medieval costume hauled on the oars as they crossed the glittering water.

Franco had hired a magnificent vessel, big enough for thirty people; he leaned over the side enjoying the procession as it glided over the lagoon to the Lido island. There they were joined by an even more magnificent boat, known as the *Serenissima*.

Once the Doge of Venice had performed the ceremony of tossing a golden ring into the water, intoning in Latin, *'Desponsamus te, Mare, in signum veri perpetique dominii.'*

'I marry you, O sea, as a sign of permanent dominium.'

Now the ceremony was performed by the mayor. Cheers went up as he made the triumphant declaration.

A few feet away Charlotte could see Franco's son and his fiancée, gazing into each other's eyes.

*'Presto,'* he said joyously. *'Presto mi sposera.'*

'They were going to marry in autumn,' Franco confided. 'But now he's pressing her to marry him quickly. That's the effect this ceremony can have. It makes people long for their own marriage.'

He turned away, calling to his other guests.

'Perhaps he's got a point,' Lucio observed.

'How do you mean?'

'Maybe it's time we were talking about marriage. We agreed that when you'd been here for a while you'd make a decision about staying. I can't believe you want to go away. You've fitted in from the beginning. Everyone likes you and they're all eagerly waiting for the announcement of our forthcoming marriage. Perhaps we should give it to them.'

So that was his idea of a proposal, she thought. After the night they'd shared she'd expected something that at least acknowledged their shared passion. Instead there was reasoned logic and efficiency.

'Only if we actually decide to marry,' she said. 'I don't remember us doing that.'

'Sorry. Where are my manners? Charlotte, I want to marry you. I think we can have a good life together, not just because of our baby, but because you really belong here. You've felt that, too, haven't you?'

'It's true that I like it here. As you say, I've been made welcome and people are kind. But there's more to marriage than that.'

'Of course there is. A man and a woman have to go well together, and we do.'

'Yes, we're good friends,' she said wryly.

'That's important. The strongest couples can be the ones who started out knowing they could rely on each other. You know how deeply I trust you. We spoke of it last night. Surely you remember that?'

'Yes,' she murmured. 'I remember last night.'

'So do I, and there were things about it that mean the world to me. There's such freedom in being able to talk to you. You know things about me that nobody else knows, or ever will, and I'm so glad. And I hope you have the same feeling that you can rely on me.

'Do you think I won't work to make you happy? I promise that I will. Anything you want, if it's humanly possible I'll see that you get it.'

*Anything I want,* she thought wryly. *Your heart? Your love? But you're telling me they wouldn't be humanly possible.*

How had this happened? Only a little time ago she'd vowed to be satisfied with their close friendship and not ask for more until later. Simple common sense.

Common sense hurt more than she'd suspected, but now she realised sadly that it was all she had. And it wasn't enough.

'Don't rush me, Lucio,' she said. 'I know we've talked about where this road is leading, but I'm not sure yet.'

He looked astounded, and she understood. How could she refuse him after last night? She didn't comprehend it herself. She only knew that she wouldn't be rushed into handing over her life to a man whose feelings fell short of hers.

'We'll talk about it later,' she said.

'All right. When we get home tonight.'

'No, I meant in a few weeks.'

His face grew tense. 'Last night you promised to always to be there for me.'

She wished he hadn't said that. The memory was so painful that she winced. He saw it and misunderstood.

'I see,' he said with a touch of bitterness. 'You regret it already.'

'No, I don't, but we were talking of friendship. As a friend, and the mother of your child, I'll never entirely leave you but I still need some independence. Just how much I need I'm not sure.'

'Come along!' That was Franco, coming towards them to sweep them back up into the festivities. 'We still have a wonderful day before us.'

'I'm not sure how long we can stay,' Charlotte faltered.

'But you must see the races,' Franco protested.

'And after that we must return,' Lucio said. 'We're grateful for your hospitality, but I have urgent things to attend to at home. I'll arrange matters through my lawyer, and come back soon to sign papers.'

For the rest of the day they smiled and said what was appropriate before travelling back across the lagoon. All around them Venice was enjoying colourful celebrations, but they could take no part. Hurrying back to the hotel they packed and prepared to leave. A motorboat was hired to take them to Piazzale Roma, and there they collected the car and drove across the bridge to the mainland.

As they drove back to Tuscany in the twilight Charlotte gazed out of the window and wondered at herself. She'd been offered so much that she longed for, yet without warning her old rebelliousness had come alive, saying that it wasn't good enough. Perhaps she had devastated the rest of her life. Maybe the day would dawn when she cursed herself for being unrealistic.

But it made no difference. The streak of sheer cussedness that had always intervened at inappropriate moments had cropped up now.

And, most incredible of all, she had no regrets.

\* \* \*

For the next few weeks they saw little of each other. Lucio spent much time at distant vineyards and for once it was a relief to Charlotte that he wasn't there.

When he came home he behaved courteously, constantly asking after her health, patting her growing bulge protectively and accompanying her on a check-up visit to the doctor. Wryly she recalled a friend back home whose husband distanced himself from the details of her pregnancy. When she protested at his lack of emotional support he was astounded. He gave her plenty of money, didn't he? The rest was 'women's stuff'.

*She would really envy me,* Charlotte thought wryly. *Lucio is everything her husband isn't: kind, attentive, interested, concerned.*

And yet—and yet…

She tried to distract herself by going online to talk to her family, and found Matt putting a call through to her. It was good to see his face on the screen. In the past she had often found more comfort in his presence than with her sisters. They were alike in many ways, sharing jokes, standing back and taking the same ironic view of life. She could tell him what had happened, and count on him to be supportive.

But this time his support took a more detached stance than she had expected.

'Ellie told me she was worried that this guy hasn't proposed to you. Now you're telling me that he did propose and you turned him down. Are you nuts?'

'I didn't turn him down. I just said we could talk about it later.'

'Listen, there are ways and ways of rejecting someone, and saying you'll talk later is one of the best known. You're nuts about him, you admit that, yet you're tak-

ing the risk of losing him altogether. Why? Because he
didn't say all the right words and you want to kick him
in the teeth.'

'That wasn't it. Truly, Matt, I wasn't just being awkward—'

'Oh, I reckon you were. As long as I've known you,
you've been famous for awkwardness. You could get a
medal for it. How many times have I rescued you from
your own foolishness?'

'About as often as I've rescued you.'

'OK. Check. But now it's *me* riding to *your* rescue. I
don't want to see you break your heart because you're
too stubborn to admit you're an idiot.'

'All right, all *right*! I admit it. But what can I do?'

'You'll have to work that out for yourself, but whatever it is, act fast. Time isn't on your side.'

'I know that,' she said, patting her stomach.

'I don't just mean the baby, although it's true your time
for playing the seductress is running out.'

'Thanks!'

'I'm talking practicalities. You're not Italian, so if you
want to marry in Italy you'll need to produce a moun-
tain of paperwork, starting with your birth certificate.'

'Oh, heavens! I never thought of that.'

'Time to be practical, decide if you really want to
marry him and, if so, get things organised.'

'Yes, I guess you're right.'

'Let me know what happens.'

However blunt his words she knew Matt had spoken
out of concern for her. *He's right,* she thought. *If I lose
Lucio it's all my own fault. I played it so stupidly but I
couldn't help it. I gambled on all or nothing and it looks
like I'm going to get nothing. It's going to take a miracle*

*to bring us together, and miracles don't seem to happen any more.*

If only Lucio was here now and she could say everything she was feeling. But another two weeks passed while he stayed away. She used the time investigating the other part of Matt's warning, and found it to be alarmingly accurate.

On the day Lucio was expected home he was late. She stood at her window, desperately looking for him, and as soon as she saw him she realised that something was up. He was driving faster than usual, and when he parked the car he leapt out, looked up at the window and ran inside.

'All right,' he said, coming into her room. 'Enough's enough. I've been doing a lot of thinking on the way home, and you've played too many games with me. I want an answer.'

'I'm not playing games—'

'Then give me an answer and make it yes.' He grasped her arm. 'Charlotte, I mean it. You've driven me to distraction and I can't take any more. I know I made a mess of the proposal. I'm not the kind of man who can go down on one knee, but I asked you because I really want you.'

'Lucio, I—*aargh!*' She broke off in a gasp.

'What is it?' he cried. 'Charlotte what happened? Did I hurt you? I didn't mean to—I barely touched you.'

'No, you didn't hurt me,' she said in a dazed voice. *'Aaah!'* She gasped again.

'What happened?' he demanded, in agony.

'The baby—it's moving. It kicked me. There! It's done it again.'

'You mean—?'

She looked down, running her fingers over her slight bulge. 'Just there. You can feel the movement from the outside.'

Tentatively, almost fearfully, he touched the bulge with his fingertips.

'Can you feel it?' she asked.

'No—yes—I think. But is it all right? Should that be happening?'

'Of course. I've felt movement before but not as much as this. It's good. It means our child is strong and healthy. It'll have a good start in the world.'

With a sigh that was almost a groan he knelt so that he could lay his head against her. He kept it there, not moving for a few moments. Then he raised his face far enough for her to see his closed eyes and gentle, ecstatic smile.

'Yes,' he whispered ecstatically. 'I can feel it—*yes*.'

He opened his eyes to see her looking down at him.

'Yes,' he repeated. 'It's wonderful.'

'Yes,' she agreed, taking his face between her hands.

'Charlotte—please—'

'Yes,' she repeated.

'You don't understand what I'm saying....'

'But I do.' She held his gaze for a moment. 'And my answer is yes.'

He rose, looking at her intently. 'You mean it?'

'Yes.'

'Marriage?'

'*Yes.*'

He put his arms around her, drawing her a little closer, but giving her extra room for the bulge.

'We're going to have a child,' he said in a dazed voice. 'I already knew that but...suddenly it's more real.'

That was also how she felt. She'd longed for a miracle, and it had been given to her. Now they had shared this moment no power on earth could have made her refuse him. Filled with contentment she rested her head on his shoulder, then tensed as there was another kick.

'Ah!' she gasped.

'Does it hurt?' he asked, full of tender anxiety for her.

'No, it just means our offspring is establishing a personality already. It's probably a boy. With a kick like that he's going to be a soccer player.'

'Or a politician,' Lucio said with a wry smile. 'He already knows how to get the better of people. Remember I said I couldn't go down on one knee?'

'And he made you do just that,' she said. 'Your first trial of strength and he won.'

He hugged her. 'I'm really looking forward to meeting this lad. Come on, let's tell everyone.'

He led her out of the bedroom and down the stairs, holding her gently but firmly.

'Be careful,' he said.

'Lucio I've used these stairs a hundred times without an accident.'

'I know but…it's different now.'

'Yes, it is,' she said, taking his hand and smiling happily.

Downstairs they told Fiorella, who went into ecstasies.

'We must arrange everything as soon as possible,' she said. 'Charlotte, my dear, have you told your family that you're getting married?'

'No, we wanted to tell you first. I'll email them, and later we'll go online and talk.'

'And then you can introduce us. We will all meet as one big happy family.'

'We can't do it all at once. My family live a long way apart, Ellie in Texas and my parents in New York, Matt in Boston and Alex in Australia. I could tell Matt and Ellie now. We're only five hours ahead of them.'

She fetched her laptop, set it up and connected to the

program that provided the video link. A glance at her list of contacts showed that neither Matt nor Ellie was online.

'No problem,' she said. 'I'll email them, tell them the news and say let's talk face to face.'

'But if they live miles apart how can you get them together?' Fiorella asked.

'They won't really be together but I can put them on the screen at the same time,' Charlotte said. 'There, the emails are on their way. If they receive them soon they'll come online without delay.'

After a few moments an email arrived announcing that Alex was away today but would be back by evening.

'Her evening,' Charlotte said. 'We'll all be asleep by then. But I'll find a way to contact her soon. Ah, I think that's Matt.'

Sure enough a flashing light was announcing Matt's arrival on screen.

'Did you really write what I thought you wrote?' he demanded. 'You're getting married?'

'Yes, and this is Lucio, my fiancé,' Charlotte said, speaking quickly in case Matt should say something that would reveal his earlier advice.

But he was tact itself, congratulating them both. Everything went well. Courtesies were exchanged. Lucio introduced his mother. Then a bleep announced that Ellie had made contact and she, too, arrived on screen, smiling and pleasant.

When all the introductions had been made again Ellie said, 'So now you've got to come to Larkville, Charlotte, and of course Lucio will come with you.'

'They're celebrating Clay Calhoun's life in October,' Charlotte explained to Lucio.

'Matt and I are invited because he was our father,'

Ellie said, 'but they want you and Alex there so we can all be together.'

'But I told you, I'll be giving birth about then,' Charlotte said. 'I'd love to come, but it won't be possible. Such a shame.'

'You might give birth early,' Ellie protested. 'Promise you'll come if you can.'

'If I can,' Charlotte agreed. She could sense that this conversation troubled Lucio and was eager to bring it to a close.

More smiles, congratulations, good wishes, and the links were closed down.

'It's nice that they want us to go over there,' Charlotte said. 'But I don't think it will be very practical.' She looked down at the bulge.

'It's not just that,' Lucio said. 'If you do go, it'll have to be without me. October is when we harvest the grapes. I couldn't possibly leave here.'

'Of course not,' she said. 'And I couldn't leave either, even if I'd already given birth. It would be too soon. Don't worry, it's not going to arise.'

His brow cleared. 'I hope not. I'd hate to refuse you the first thing you've asked me.'

'So now we have a lot of talking to do,' Fiorella declared. 'You must set the date, send out the invitations. How soon can we make it happen? How about the week after next.'

'I'm afraid not,' Lucio said. 'Because Charlotte wasn't born here we have to get a lot of paperwork—her birth certificate, a sworn declaration that she's free to marry which must be translated, annotated and taken round a load of offices. It can take a few weeks.'

Charlotte stared. This was what she'd been preparing to tell him, but he already knew.

'Oh, what a pity,' Fiorella mourned. 'Well, you'd better get to work on all those papers, and we'll have the wedding as soon as possible.'

She bustled away, full of plans.

'I know what you're thinking.' Lucio sighed. 'How do I know all this? I must have been checking up, which means I took it for granted that you'd say yes. Or I was planning to pressure you, which makes me all sorts of an undesirable character. It's not like that, Charlotte, truly. I just wanted to be ready for anything. Don't be angry with me.'

'Have you finished? Then listen to what I have to say. I know about all these formalities and how long they can take, and I've been doing something about it. Matt's already sent me the birth certificate and a sworn statement that I'd never been married.'

'You've been doing all that?' Lucio breathed.

'Yes. There's still some work left to do….'

'But you did this? So you meant to marry me?'

'I suppose I did. I've got as much ready as I can, but there's still some—'

She broke off as he seized her in his arms, and after that there were no more words.

Two days later he drove her into Florence.

'There's something I want to show you,' he said, leading her along the street until they reached a jewellery shop and pointing to a double-stranded pearl necklace in the window. 'What do you think of that?'

'It's really beautiful.'

'Would it make a beautiful wedding present?'

'Oh, yes.'

'Let's go in.'

In the shop she tried on the necklace and loved the

way it looked on her. It was a wedding gift to make any bride happy.

'But what am I going to give you?' she asked as they left the shop.

He glanced down at her waist.

'You're already giving me the best gift in the world,' he said. 'I don't need anything else.'

She knew a burst of happiness. Everything was going to be all right, after all.

# CHAPTER ELEVEN

For the next two weeks they were seldom out of each other's company, travelling from office to office, presenting documents, signing paperwork.

'So now everything's in order,' she said as they sat in a café, having just left the American consulate in Florence. 'Everything signed, every permission granted. The perfect business deal.'

'I wish I could say you were wrong—' he grinned '—but I've had commercial ventures that were less complex than this.'

'You can't blame them for being careful about foreigners,' she pointed out. 'I might have a dozen ex-husbands back in the States.'

'I'm not even going to ask you about that. I recognise one of your wicked moods. You'd enjoy freezing me with terror.'

'Well, anyway, we made it to the end, and we're all set for the business deal of the century. Shake?'

'Shake.' He took her extended hand.

She often teased him like this these days. It saved her from the embarrassment of making it obvious that her feelings were stronger and deeper than his.

It wasn't the kind of wedding a woman would dream of, especially with a man she loved. But it was better than parting from him. Inwardly she sent a silent message of gratitude to Matt, who had alerted her to danger in good time.

When everything was sorted they opted for a speedy marriage on the first available date. Instead of the huge array of business contacts that would normally have revelled in the public relations, only the very closest friends were invited.

Fiorella helped her choose a wedding gift for Lucio, using her knowledge of him to direct Charlotte to a valuable collection of books about the history of the wine industry. To add a more personal touch she bought a vest with the logo of the local soccer team, and wrote a note saying, 'You can give him this when he's ready.'

It was settled between them now that she was to bear a son who would make his name in some profession where his mighty kick would give him an advantage. When Lucio opened the parcel his delighted grin told her that he understood the joke. His hug was fierce and appreciative.

'We haven't discussed a honeymoon yet,' he reminded her.

'It's not really the right time, is it? Let's wait until after October when the harvest is in.'

He kissed her. 'You're going to be a great vintner's wife. But have a think about the honeymoon, too.'

In fact, she already knew where she wanted to go for their honeymoon, but she would wait for the right time to tell him.

The big disappointment was that none of her family could come to Tuscany for the wedding.

'Your father isn't well enough to make the journey,' her mother said. 'And I can't leave him alone.'

'Oh, I wish I could come,' Alex said.

'But Australia's so far away.' Charlotte sighed.

Ellie and Matt were also too tied up with events in their own lives. There was a triumphant video link during which they toasted Lucio and Charlotte, who raised their glasses in return.

'But it's not the same as seeing them,' Charlotte sighed to Lucio afterwards.

'No, it would have given you the chance to feel part of the family again,' he said. 'But there'll be another chance. There has to be.'

'I don't see how. Going to Larkville in October would have been a good chance because everyone will be there together, but that's out of the question. I'll be giving birth, and even if I'm not, *you'll* be giving birth.'

'*Eh?*'

'To a grape harvest.'

'Oh, I see. Yes, I suppose it is a bit like producing an offspring, being a proud father—'

'Telling the world that your creation is better than the next father's?' she suggested.

'Right. Or letting the world find out for itself.'

'Which it'll do at our wedding reception,' she said lightly.

But he wasn't fooled by her attempt to put a brave face on things.

'I'm really sorry your family can't be there. I wish there was something I could do.'

'But even you can't tell the grapes to wait another couple of weeks,' she said lightly. 'I'll get over it. Thanks anyway. Now get outta here. I'm going to put on my party dress and I don't want you to see it first.'

Although there would be no lavish reception there was a small party three nights before the wedding. Chief among the guests was Franco, who clearly felt he could take some credit for bringing the wedding about, and made a theatrical speech.

'What is life without love?' he demanded. 'There is no more beautiful sight in the world than two people deeply in love, vowing fidelity to each other. Together they will face the challenges that the world will throw at them, and because they are united they will be strong. Because they are one in heart they will achieve victory.

'My friends, a couple in love is an inspiration to us all.' He raised his glass. 'Let us toast them.'

Everybody rose, lifting their glasses and uttering congratulations. Lucio rose also, raising his glass to her. She responded in the same way, managing to look blissfully happy, and refusing to heed the irony in the speech. Lucio was her promised husband, as she was his promised wife. Together they would play the role of devoted lovers.

Somebody struck up on the piano, and there was dancing. The guests roared their appreciation as Lucio led her onto the floor and took her into his arms for a slow, dreamy waltz.

'You look beautiful,' he said. 'That's a lovely dress.'

'Thank you.'

'I'm wearing something special, too.'

'Yes, you look very handsome in that dinner jacket.'

'I don't mean that. I mean underneath. Look.'

He released her hand and slipped his fingers into the front of his shirt, pulling the edges apart just far enough for her to see—

'The soccer vest!' she exclaimed. 'You're wearing it.'

'It's the cleverest gift you could have bought me. I wear it in honour of you, and of him.'

'Oh, you—' She began to laugh. 'Of all the things to—honestly!'

Now he, too, was laughing, drawing her closer so that

she laid her head against him and together they shook
with amusement. All around them their guests sighed
with pleasure, for surely nobody had ever seen a couple
so deeply in love.

'You don't mind if I vanish for a stag night?' Lucio had
asked her.

Since he was already attired for an evening out the
question was purely rhetorical.

'I'm tempted to say yes I mind a lot, just to see what
you'd do,' she teased. 'Don't be silly, of course you must
have a stag night. You don't want people to think you're
henpecked, do you? Not yet anyway.'

'Yes, we'll wait a decent interval before you crack the
whip,' he said, grinning.

'Oh, you think that's a joke, do you?' She pointed to
the door and said theatrically, 'Get out of here at once!'

'Yes, ma'am, no, ma'am.' He saluted and hurried out
to the car where his friends were waiting. She waved him
off, thinking that these were the best moments between
them, for now they were most completely in tune.

She was awoken in the early hours by the sound of the
car arriving outside, and went hurriedly down to open
the door. Having delivered him safely his friends said
farewell and drove off.

For a man returning from a stag night he seemed rela-
tively sober, although sleepy, and he regarded the stairs
with dismay.

'I'll help you up them,' she said.

Together they managed to reach the top, but there he
clutched the railing and murmured, 'I don't think I can
go any farther.'

'Never mind. You can sleep in my room. It's just here.
Come on.'

She got him as far as the bed where he dropped down with relief.

'Did you enjoy yourself?' she asked.

'Mmm!'

'Good. That's all that matters.'

He turned his head on the pillow. 'You're a very understanding woman.'

'If I'm going to marry you I'll need to be.'

'Mmm!'

'Go to sleep.' She chuckled.

His eyes were already closed, and he was breathing deeply. She watched him tenderly for a moment, then leaned down and kissed him on the mouth.

'Sleep well, and don't worry about anything,' she said.

Still without opening his eyes he moved his arms so that they enfolded her, drawing her close. Happily she snuggled up, her head on his shoulder.

'Mmm!' he said again.

'Mmm!' she agreed.

'I'm sorry,' he murmured.

'No need.'

'The baby.' He sighed. 'I feel guilty.'

'There's nothing to feel guilty about,' she assured him.

His next words came in such a soft whisper that she had to lean closer to hear it. What she heard made her tense, wondering if she'd misheard, for surely it wasn't possible—surely…?

'I wasn't fair,' he murmured. 'You wanted to wait until we were married…I wouldn't listen…forgive me—'

'But back then we weren't—'

'I begged and begged until you gave in…not fair…but when we're married, nobody will know that we…our secret…our secret. Say you forgive me.'

She took a deep breath, summoning her resolve. She

didn't want to do what she was about to, but there was no choice if he was to have peace.

'There's nothing to forgive, my darling,' she assured him. 'I want you as much as you want me. We love each other, and we'll be married soon.'

She had known about the burden he carried, blaming himself for Maria's death. Now she knew there had been another burden all along, one which haunted him, sleeping and waking.

They had been lovers, and Maria had conceived his child. Doubtless her pregnancy had been in the very early days, so nobody else suspected, and the truth could be hidden until after the wedding. But she had died, and the child had died with her. There had been nobody he could tell, and even now he staggered under a terrifying sense of guilt.

'Dead,' he was murmuring, 'my fault.'

'*No!*' she said fiercely. 'None of it is your fault.'

But she despaired of convincing him. She'd known that he was haunted by the fear that he had inadvertently killed Maria. Now she saw that his feeling of guilt and self-blame extended to the death of his first unborn child. It was wildly unlikely and illogical, but it shed a new light over his protectiveness towards her, his fear of making love.

The thought of his suffering made her weep, and she held him tenderly against her.

He stirred, clasping her more tightly. 'Are you there?'

'Yes, I'm here. Hold on to me, and go to sleep, my darling.'

He sighed and she felt the tension drain out of him. Now he was at peace, and all was well as long as she was there for him. She held him gently until they both fell asleep.

She awoke first, to find that neither of them had moved in two hours. His eyes were still closed, but as she watched they opened slowly. For a moment his expression was vague, but then he smiled as though something had eased his mind.

'So much for a macho stag night,' he said.

'As long as you enjoyed yourself, what else matters?'

He eased himself up, moving carefully.

'I'm sorry,' he said. 'I had no right to bother you while I was in that state.'

'What state? You didn't do anything objectionable. You just couldn't stay awake.'

'I probably talked a lot of nonsense.'

'Not a thing. Stop worrying.'

He made his way to the door, but looked back, seeming troubled.

'I didn't…say anything, did I?'

'Not that I remember. Bye.'

He hesitated a moment. 'Bye.'

He gave her a final look, and quietly departed.

The words were there in his mind, she thought, but he wasn't sure if it was a memory or a dream. Let him think of it as a dream. That would be easier for him.

In the beginning loving him had seemed simple. Now she knew it wasn't going to be simple at all.

But she had made her choice, and nothing was going to make her change it.

Franco was going to give the bride away. He arrived just as Lucio was about to leave for the church, slapped him on the shoulder and told him to be off. Then he ushered the bride out to his chauffeur-driven car, with Fiorella following.

'Have you got the ring?' he asked before they started.

For this marriage ceremony there were two matching rings, which the bride and groom exchanged.

'Here,' Fiorella said, holding it up. 'Everything has been taken care of.'

Everything taken care of, Charlotte mused as the car headed for Siena. But there were still so many questions unanswered, questions that might never be answered because they would never be asked.

As soon as she entered the church she could see down the aisle to where Lucio was waiting for her. Enrico gave her his arm, the organ struck up and she began to advance. As she grew closer to Lucio she could see that his eyes never left her for a moment. There was a contented look in them that filled her with pleasure, and as she neared he reached out to her, taking her hand and drawing her to his side.

The first part of the service was formal, but at last it was time to exchange rings. Slowly Lucio slid the ring on her finger, saying quietly, 'Take this ring as a sign of my love and fidelity.'

Then it was her turn. Raising his hand, she slid the ring onto it, murmuring, 'Take this ring as a sign of my love and fidelity.'

Love and fidelity.

She meant the words with all her heart. Looking up into his face she saw there an intensity of emotion that gave her a surge of joy.

The moment came. She felt his lips on hers, not passionate as she had known them, but firm and gentle. A brief trip to the sacristy to sign the register, then a return to the church where they were proclaimed husband and wife as they began the journey along the aisle, hand in hand.

*He is my husband and I am his wife. Now I belong to*

*him and he...perhaps he belongs to me—perhaps—or at least to our son.*

The rest of the day was a triumph. To Charlotte it seemed that almost everything she had wished for was coming true. Acceptance, a home, a new family.

At last it was time to retire to bed, now a shared room with Lucio. She climbed the stairs on his arm, followed him into their room and accepted his help undressing.

'I'm worn out,' she said sleepily. 'Who'd have thought getting married was so exhausting?'

'True,' he said, yawning. 'And I've got to be up early tomorrow to talk to Toni, my head steward. He's got some ideas for next year that we'll have to plan for now.'

'Goodnight,' she said.

His kissed her forehead. 'Goodnight, my dear.'

This was their wedding night.

The months moved on. Now she was glad to live a slower, more relaxed life, her thoughts always focused on the future. Eight weeks until the birth, seven, six—

'Oh, I can't bear this,' Fiorella squealed. 'We want to welcome him into the world and he keeps us waiting.'

'No, he doesn't,' Charlotte said with mock indignation. 'He's not late, it's just us that's impatient.'

'We are all impatient,' Elizabetta chimed in.

Charlotte regarded her fondly. By now she knew Elizabetta's history. As a young woman she had been married, and pregnant. But the child had been born early, at only seven months. Within a few hours it was dead, and Elizabeth, too, had nearly died. Charlotte felt that many a woman in her position would have felt resentful of another woman's luck. But Elizabetta was too generous and warm-hearted to feel bitterness towards her.

As autumn gradually appeared it was a pleasure to

sit on the terrace, watching the setting sun, drinking in the warmth.

One evening she was sitting there feeling at one with life, with the world and everyone in it. In the distance she could see a car that she recognised as Toni's. Doubtless he was on his way to make a report to Lucio. She would go inside and arrange with the kitchen staff to have his favourite coffee ready.

Exactly what happened next she was never sure, but as she passed across the tops of the steps that led down from the terrace to the ground, she felt her foot turn underneath her. She tried to grasp something to save herself but it was too late. She felt a bang as her head hit the stone railings, and the next moment she was tumbling down the stairs.

From somewhere far above she heard a scream. Then she blacked out.

# CHAPTER TWELVE

THE pain was everywhere, sweeping through her in waves. She had the strange sensation of sleeping while being racked by gusts of agony. She tried to reach out, pleading for help, but it was hard to move.

From a great distance came voices: Fiorella screaming, 'Call an ambulance!' Then Lucio crying, 'Charlotte—oh, my God, what happened? Charlotte, speak to me, please. Charlotte! *Charlotte!*'

She tried to respond but his voice faded as she blacked out. But after a while she managed to open her eyes a little, and see strangers, wearing uniforms. One of them, a woman, was saying, 'Lift her this way—careful, easy now. How did this happen? Did anyone see it?'

'She fell down the steps of the terrace and hit her head.' That was Enrico's voice. 'I saw it from a distance but, oh, heavens! I was too far away to help her.'

'My baby,' she whispered.

The strange woman's voice replied, 'We'll soon have you in the hospital. Hold on.'

She was being carried. From somewhere came the sound of doors opening, then being slammed shut, engines roaring.

'Lucio?' she cried.

'I'm here,' he said, close to her ear. His hand grasped hers. 'Can you feel me?'

'Yes, yes…'

'Can't this ambulance go any faster?' he shouted.

The woman's voice said, 'I've alerted the hospital. They're ready for her. They'll do their best to save the baby.'

'They've got to save *her*.' Lucio's cry was almost a scream. 'Don't you understand? *Her!*'

She tried to open her eyes but the blackness was sweeping over her again. It blended with the roar of the engine to create a world in which there was only fear, pain, uncertainty.

Then she was being hurried along a hospital corridor on a trolley, lifted onto a bed. A doctor and nurse regarded her anxiously, and a fierce pain convulsed her.

'The baby,' she gasped. 'I think it's coming.'

'No,' Lucio groaned. 'Please, Doctor, don't let that happen. She's so weak and hurt, it'll be too much for her.'

'If it's really started,' the doctor said, 'then there's not a lot— Stand back please.'

He leaned over Charlotte, asking her urgent questions, which she found it hard to answer with her consciousness coming and going.

'Save my baby,' she begged. '*Please*—save my baby— *Aaah!*'

Now there was no doubt that her labour had started, nearly six weeks early. The focus of her life, the child that was to unite her and Lucio on the road ahead, was in danger.

Nothing was in her control. The urge to push possessed her and she bore down, struggling against the pain, groaning.

'No,' she whispered. 'No, please—I can't do this….'

'I'm afraid you must,' the doctor said. 'But we'll do everything we can to make it easier.'

'What can *I* do?' Lucio demanded harshly.

'Be here and support her—that is, if you feel you can. Some fathers can't bear to be present during childbirth.'

'Then they ought to be shot,' Lucio snapped. 'Just try to get rid of me.'

He dropped to his knees beside Charlotte so that his face was close to hers.

'Did you hear that? I'm staying here. We're going to do this together—no, that's not really true. You're going to be doing all the hard work, I'm afraid. But I'll be here, cheering you on.'

'And him,' she whispered. 'Our little soccer star?'

'And him. Right into the goal.'

'Always on the winning side. *Aaah!*'

'That's it,' said the doctor. 'Push. Excellent.'

To brace herself against the pain she clenched her hand tighter than ever, so that Lucio gave a sharp groan at the fierceness of her grip.

'Sorry,' she gasped.

'Never mind me,' he said. 'You just worry about yourself—and him.'

Her head was aching badly. A nurse tended it, wiping away a trickle of blood. In her confusion she believed that there could be no way out of this. She was trapped in a desert of agony and dread, and there seemed no escape. She had sworn to help Lucio in every way, and if the child died it would destroy him.

But then she felt Lucio holding her, sending a message of comfort and love that seemed to reach her down the corridors of eternity. She yearned towards him, not with her hands but with her heart and soul, knowing that now he was all she had in the world.

She had no idea how long the birth took. She only knew that nothing else existed in the world. Then, after a while, the pain ceased to attack her and faded to a constant ache. Swamped by exhaustion she vaguely sensed that something was gone from inside her.

'My baby,' she whispered. 'Please—'

Lucio leaned close.

'Our daughter was born safely,' he murmured. 'She's been put into an incubator, and she'll be there for several days.'

'She's…going to live?'

'It's too soon to be certain, but they're hopeful.'

'You said…daughter.'

'Yes,' he told her gently. 'We have a little girl.'

She wanted to say something but the world faded again. Surely Lucio had wanted a son, and she had disappointed him? What would he say? What would he feel?

Now she was on fire. Heat was all around her, inside her, destroying thought and consciousness. Destroying her. Voices again, talking about fever. But one voice dominated them all.

'Charlotte, listen to me. Can you hear me, wherever you are? You must, *you must hear me*.'

'Yes, yes…'

He seemed to become more agitated.

'You've got to hang on. You've got a fever but they're giving you something for it, and you're going to be all right. You understand that? You're going to be all right, but you've got to fight. I'm here. We'll fight together. You can't go off anywhere now, not when you've made me love you so much. That would be really inconsiderate, wouldn't it? And I know you'd never do that.'

His voice grew more gentle.

'Or perhaps you don't know how much I love you.

I've never said it but you're clever enough to understand without words. Mostly I didn't understand it myself. I don't think I really knew until now, but you knew. Sure you did, because you know everything. You saw through me from the start, and let's face it, you've had me dancing to your tune.

'But you can't do that and then just vanish. You can't just abandon me. Charlotte, my love, can you hear me? *Can you hear me?*'

His voice seemed to follow her into the engulfing darkness, holding on to her, never leaving her, so that at last she felt the darkness yield and give her back to him.

'Open your eyes, darling. That's it! Look, everyone, she's awake!' Lucio's face, haggard and unshaven but full of joy, hovered above her. 'Can you see me?'

'Yes, I knew you were there,' she murmured.

'I'm still here. I always will be.'

'Our baby—?'

'She's fine. She's beautiful. The doctors say you're both doing well, but if you knew how scared I've been.'

She could believe it. He looked terrible, like a man who hadn't slept for a year.

Suddenly she remembered him as he'd been at their first meeting in Rome, just over seven months ago; wickedly handsome, vibrant, sophisticated, dominating the company with the power of his looks and personality, alive to every challenge, in control of every situation.

Now, even through several days' growth of beard, she could see lines that hadn't been there before. And his eyes told a story of agony. It was like looking at a totally different man. Who had done this cruel thing to him?

She had.

'There was no need to be scared,' she told him.

'How can you know that? If you could have seen how you looked—as though you'd already gone far ahead to a place where I couldn't reach you.'

'It's all right,' she whispered. 'That was never going to happen.'

'You can't be sure—'

'Yes, I can. I would never have left you.'

Fiorella came forward, her eyes warm and loving.

'Bless you, dearest Charlotte! Oh, it's so good to see you getting better! We were all so worried.'

Lucio had turned away to say something to a nurse. Fiorella lowered her voice.

'I thought he was going to go crazy. He's been here for days, refusing to leave you, except for a moment to see the baby. I had to bring food in to him because he wouldn't even go to the canteen.'

'Poor Lucio. He looks terrible.'

'Yes, but he'll be all right now his mind can be at rest about you.'

'He's seen the baby?'

'Yes, they couldn't bring her in here because she's in an incubator, but she's strong enough to leave it now so they'll bring her to you. If only you could have seen his face when he saw her for the first time. He wanted to take her in his arms but she had to stay in the incubator, and he was so upset. Lucio, tell Charlotte—oh, he's gone.'

While they were talking Lucio had left the room. They discovered why a moment later when he returned carrying a small bundle close to his chest. Fiorella slid out of the way so that he could sit on the bed, and discreetly glided out of the door, leaving them alone.

'Here she is,' he said. 'Our child.'

Gently he laid the tiny being against her mother's bosom, then turned his body, putting his arm behind her shoulders, supporting mother and child. Charlotte gazed down, entranced, at the tiny face. The baby's eyes were closed and she was deeply asleep, blissfully oblivious of the outside world and the anguish that her arrival had caused.

*So we meet at last,* Charlotte thought. *You're going to make everything different.*

Lucio's arms were keeping her safe. His rough, unshaven face was scratching her cheek. She turned her head to share a smile with him, receiving his answering glow before they both returned their gazes to the baby.

'Thank you,' he murmured. 'Thank you with all my heart.'

'No, thank you,' she whispered. 'You and she have given me something I never thought I'd have. Now I know I'll have it forever.'

Fiorella appeared in the doorway.

'I left because I thought you three would like to be alone for a while,' she said. 'But I must just see her.' She came over to the bed. 'She's so beautiful.'

'All this time,' Charlotte reflected, 'we were wrong about it being a son.'

'Only because we assumed that a strong baby must be male,' Lucio said. 'That was very old-fashioned of us. We forgot that females can be strong, too. The doctor says she's fit and vigorous, and she's come through that premature birth with all flags flying.' He grinned. 'You never know. She might grow up to play soccer yet. Or maybe she'll settle for ruling the world, the way she already rules ours.'

'But didn't you really want a son?'

'I told you, I didn't mind either way.'

'Yes, but I thought—'

'I know what you thought, that I was just being polite

about it. You kept telling me I wanted a boy and I just accepted what you said.' He laid a finger against the baby's cheek. 'I guess I'll just have to get used to being bossed around by my womenfolk.' He gave Fiorella a wicked grin. 'After all, I've had lots of practice.'

'It'll come in useful.' Fiorella chuckled. 'And what are you going to call your little girl?'

'We haven't thought about it yet,' Lucio said. He laid a hand on Charlotte's shoulder. 'Do you have any ideas?'

'Yes,' she said. 'I want to call her Maria.'

Fiorella made a sudden movement, pleased but uncertain.

'You will name her after my girl?' she breathed. 'That is wonderful but, Charlotte, are you sure? Why do you do this? If it is kindness for me, I thank you, but please do not force yourself.'

'I'm not forcing myself,' she said. 'It's what I want to do.'

She looked at Lucio, who was watching her in stunned silence. Fiorella also saw his expression, understood it and slipped quietly out of the room.

'Forgive me if I don't know what to say,' he murmured. 'This is the last thing I expected. I don't know why you— but is Fiorella right? Is this an act of generosity because, if it is, you can't think I'd ever ask you to—'

'I know you wouldn't,' she said when he stumbled to a halt. 'This is what I want.'

'But why? Are you afraid of her? Do you think I love her and not you?'

'My darling, you've got it all wrong. I don't fear Maria as a rival. I did once, but now I know that she was one part of your life, and I'm another. Keep her in your heart. Go on loving her. She doesn't threaten me. I don't want to get rid of her, either from your life or mine.'

He was staring at her as though he couldn't believe what he heard. Far back in his eyes she saw joy warring with something that was almost fear.

'And my love for you,' he stammered, 'tell me you believe in it, I beg you.'

'I didn't believe it for a long time. I knew you wanted to be a father, have the family we can make together.' She touched his face. 'I knew she was pregnant when she died. You told me when you came back from your stag night. You weren't in your right mind and you thought you were talking to her. Gradually I realised what you meant.'

He groaned and hung his head. 'I wondered next day—I couldn't be sure.'

'You could always have told me.'

'I meant to. I just didn't want to have any secrets from you, and I longed to tell you everything, but I was afraid you'd take it the wrong way. You might have felt insulted, or thought I was making you second best.'

'That was true once. There was a time when I felt you were just "making do" with me.'

'And you didn't sock me on the jaw? Why not? I deserved it.'

'I loved you. I didn't feel I had the right to blame you for not being in love with me. You can't love to order. I hoped we'd grow closer in time and then—who knows?'

'Yes, it took me too long to understand my own heart,' he said sombrely. 'It might have taken longer if you hadn't been in danger during the birth. Then it became hideously clear to me that if you died my own life was over. Nothing mattered but you.'

'And our baby,' she said softly.

He met her eyes and shook his head slightly. 'You,' he said. 'Just you.'

Without waiting for her reply he laid his head down on the pillow beside her.

'You make me complete and you keep me safe,' he murmured. 'I never knew before how much I needed that. But now I know, and I'll never let you go. I warn you, I'll be possessive, domineering, practically making a prisoner of you. Don't think I'll ever let you escape me, because I won't. You'll probably get very fed up with my behaviour.'

She enfolded him in her arms and he buried his face against her.

'I think I can just about manage to put up with you,' she whispered.

A week later mother and baby returned home and Charlotte entered a stage of life more beautiful than anything she could have imagined. Her strength returned quickly, her relationship with her child flowered.

She had the pleasure of seeing Lucio completely happy now that both his personal and professional lives were reaching a triumphant peak. Harvest time was approaching, and everyone was studying the grapes intently to pick exactly the right moment. Testing was under way to determine the levels of sugar, acid and tannin.

'At one time there was only one way to find out,' Lucio told her. 'And that was to put the grapes in your mouth. Nowadays there are machines that will do some of it, but there's still no substitute for what your own taste buds tell you. Mine tell me it'll need a few more days, but then I'll unleash my workers on the vines.'

While many vintners used machines for the harvest Lucio still preferred to have his grapes picked by humans. It made him popular in the area where the employment he offered was a godsend to many. Already the temporary workers were appearing on the estate, waiting for the signal to start.

Charlotte's other great pleasure came from the delight of her family over the birth of their newest member. They squealed with delight when she held up baby Maria so that she could be seen via the video link.

'Oh, I do wish you were coming to Larkville,' Ellie sighed one night. 'You and Lucio and Maria. We're all so miserable at not being able to get over there for your wedding or the christening, and if you all came to Larkville it would really bind the family together.'

'I know,' Charlotte said, supressing a sigh. 'I really wish I could come, Ellie, honestly I do. But the harvest is about to start.'

'But why do you have to be there for the harvest?' Ellie asked. 'Surely they can do it without you?'

'Well, I won't actually be picking grapes,' she agreed. 'But I won't leave Lucio for the first harvest of our marriage. It's a great moment for him, and I must share it with him.'

'Would he really stop you coming here?'

'No, he wouldn't. He's too generous. But I wouldn't be so unfair as to ask him. I want to be here to share the harvest with him. It'll mean the world to me.'

'More than your family?'

'Lucio is my family now.'

'All right, you do what you think right. We'll be able to talk again tomorrow, then I have to be off to the airport.'

Charlotte shut down the link and sat for a moment thinking about what she had just done. It was a final choice, she knew that. Nor did she regret it for a moment. In Lucio she had gained more than she could have hoped for in a thousand years.

Smiling, she raised Maria in her arms and went to find him. Only to discover that he had just left the house.

'I don't know what got into him,' Fiorella said. 'I thought he was home for the day but he suddenly remembered something he had to do, and took off. Look, you can see his car in the distance. Men can be so annoying!'

Lucio returned a couple of hours later, coming upon Charlotte just as she was putting Maria to bed. Despite Maria being only a few weeks old there was no doubt that her eyes brightened at the sight of her father.

'It's lucky I'm not easily jealous,' Charlotte said. 'Or I might object to having to struggle for her attention.'

'Yes, Fiorella does try to come first with her.' Lucio grinned.

'Actually, I meant you. It's supposed to be the mother who gets up to look after her at night.'

'You mean last night? Well, I brought her to you, didn't I?'

'Only because I'm breastfeeding her. That's one thing you haven't been able to take over. It's lucky the harvest will be starting soon, and that will take up your attention.'

'Actually, it won't,' he said slowly. 'I'm going to let Toni take over the harvest, because I won't be here.'

'Won't—? But where will you be?'

He positioned himself to get a good look at her face before saying, 'I'll be in Larkville, with you and Maria.'

'But I—'

'I've checked with the doctor. He says it's OK for both of you to travel. And I know you want to go because I eavesdropped on the video link you had with Ellie yesterday.'

'You what?'

'And I'm glad I did. I learned a lot from listening to you, and it was very clear to me what I had to do. I've spent this afternoon talking to Toni, my overseer, and some of the others, about what to do while I'm away. They're delighted. They're all too experienced to need me.'

'But the harvest—I know what it means to you to be here.'

'And I know what it means to you to reconcile with your family and to meet your other family. There'll never be another chance as perfect as this, and you simply have to take it.'

He grasped her in urgent hands.

'Listen to me, Charlotte. I've told you that I love you, but I haven't proved it. They were just words, easy to say.'

'But I believe them.'

'And you're right. But the time will come when you'll ask yourself what I ever gave up for you, and I don't want the answer to be "nothing". So far all I've done is take. Now it's time for you to take and me to give.'

'Oh, Lucio—Lucio…'

'Come here.'

His mouth on hers was firm and gentle, assertive but pleading—a mixture of the feelings and attitudes around which their love was built.

'Now,' he said when he'd released her, 'get on to the computer and tell them we're coming. All of us. You, me and Maria.'

'Lucio, are you sure?'

'I was never more sure of anything in my life.'

With all her heart she longed to believe that he meant it, but still a little doubt remained. At the last minute he would realise the size of the undertaking he'd committed himself to, and realise that it was impossible.

These thoughts went through her head as they travelled to the Florence airport, to board the plane to Texas, accompanied by Fiorella. Every moment Charlotte expected him to say something, to back off, count on her understanding. But nothing happened.

*It's down to me,* she thought at last. *I must tell him that there's no need for this. I'll release him. I must.*

As they neared Passport Control she took a deep breath. 'Lucio—'

'Just a minute,' he said. 'There's my cell phone. *Toni!*'

So that was it, she thought. Toni had called to tell him they couldn't manage without him, and he must return at once. She listened to what Lucio was saying.

'Right…. Good…. So that's fine then. Thanks for telling me. Now I can really enjoy myself in the States. See you in a few days.' He hung up. 'Right now, are we ready? Goodbye, Mamma. I'll call you when we get there. Darling, is something the matter? You look strange.'

'No, I—I can hardly believe this is happening.'

'You'd better believe it. Off we go!'

And suddenly all the questions were answered. They were going through Passport Control, down the corridor into the departure lounge and onto the plane. Then it was time for take-off.

Lucio had prepared for the long flight by buying the best seats, and urging Charlotte to sit by the window.

Lying back, her child in her arms, her beloved at her side, Charlotte was able to look out on the clouds that separated her from the earth, and relish the sensation of being in another universe, one where everything was perfect.

'Maria's getting restless,' Lucio said at last. 'I think she wants to be fed.'

He moved, turning his body so that it formed a protective barrier between Charlotte and anyone who might pass down the aisle.

'Thank you,' she said happily. 'And we've got the

seats in two rows all to ourselves, haven't we? What a lucky chance that nobody else wanted them. Why are you laughing like that?'

'It's not chance. I bought eight seats.'

'You—you did what? You bought all these seats?'

'So that you'd have privacy when you needed it.'

'You thought of that?' she whispered.

'I think of you every moment. I long for you to ask me for something, so that I can have the pleasure of giving it to you and showing you what you are to me.'

'Well…there is something.'

'Yes?' And the eagerness in his face told her that he spoke truly when he said he wanted to please her.

'That vineyard in Veneto, I loved the house. Now you've bought it, could it be our home? I know you'll still have to spend some time in Tuscany for Fiorella's sake—'

'But that place will be our main home. Yours and mine. You're right. In fact, you've given me an idea.'

'What?'

'Wait and see.'

They sat in silence, watching the child take nourishment from her mother, looking up at her with eyes filled with contentment.

'She feels safe,' Lucio said. 'Everyone who knows you feels safe.'

'But not only safe, surely?' she asked.

'We'll talk about that later, when you've completely recovered.'

She smiled. Lucio's protective side had been in full flood since the birth, for both herself and Maria.

'I still can't believe you let me make this trip,' she said.

'I didn't *let* you do it,' he corrected her gently. 'I *made* you do it, because you needed to. And whatever you need is what I want.'

He was right in everything, she reflected. Because of his sacrifice she could believe in his love as never before. And he had understood that. It was the final proof of all that she needed to know.

Looking out of the window she saw that the clouds were clearing, and the world was full of sunshine.

*Rome: four months later*

Against the darkness the lights glittered on the rushing water. Everywhere there was music, people laughing and singing as they crowded around the Trevi Fountain. Coins were spun into the water, and a thousand wishes rose into the air.

'Have you guessed why I wanted to return to Rome for our honeymoon?' Charlotte asked as they made their way into the square.

'I thought it might have something to do with the last time we were here,' Lucio replied. 'Exactly one year ago today.'

'Yes, we sat at that little café over there, and we talked. Oh, how we talked!'

'And then we went to the fountain. You threw in a coin and cried, "Bring me back to Rome".'

'And I got my wish,' she said. 'Because here I am, with you. That was what I wanted then, what I want now, what I'll always want for the rest of our lives.'

'Who could have foreseen what lay ahead of us?' he marvelled. 'We thought we'd know each other for just a few hours. But that night, our whole futures were decided by a kindly fate.'

'Kindly?' she asked with just a hint of teasing. 'Are you sure?'

'You know better than to ask me that.'

She chuckled. 'You weren't so certain when Maria's milk landed all over your shirt when you'd just got dressed for the evening.'

'She can do anything she likes and it's fine by me. You have to expect the unexpected.'

'And it's certainly been unexpected,' she mused.

'Right. That first night, who'd have thought that a year later you'd have her and me.'

'Not to mention finding myself the owner of a Veneto vineyard,' she mused.

'A man should give his wife a nice wedding present. Like you said, that will always be our real home. I'm glad you like it.'

'If I listed all the things about you that I like we'd be here forever.'

He held out his hand. 'Come on, let's go and tell Oceanus that he got it right.'

There was the stone deity, dominating the fountain, arrogantly accepting all the coins that were tossed at his feet.

'What happens to the coins?' Charlotte wondered.

'They're regularly gathered up and put into a fund for the needy,' Lucio explained. 'So it's a good way of saying thank-you for a thousand blessings.'

From his pocket he pulled out a bag, heavy with high-value coins, which he shared with her. Together they tossed coin after coin into the water.

'Bring us back to Rome,' he cried.

'Next year,' she added, 'and the year after.'

'And again and again,' he called. 'Do you hear that? Bring us back.'

'Bring us back,' she echoed.

Lucio put his arm about her, looking down at her with adoration.

'But it must be together,' he said. 'Because together is what we always want to be.'

Slowly she nodded. 'Yes,' she murmured. 'Yes.'

There was no need to say more. Everything had been said, enough for the rest of their lives. In the shining light of the fountain he laid his lips on hers for a kiss that was a herald of the night to come, and the years to come. Then, arms about each other, they walked away.

\* \* \* \* \*

**COMING NEXT MONTH from Harlequin® Romance**
AVAILABLE JANUARY 2, 2013

### #4357 THE HEIR'S PROPOSAL
**Raye Morgan**
Tori was the butler's daughter, Marc the heir. He's still out of her league, but can being unexpectedly thrown together lead to second chances?

### #4358 THE SOLDIER'S SWEETHEART
*The Larkville Legacy*
**Soraya Lane**
When Nate left Sarah, he broke her heart. But now he's back in Larkville. After all that's happened, there's still that spark between them....

### #4359 THE BILLIONAIRE'S FAIR LADY
**Barbara Wallace**
When Manhattan heiress Roxy enlists the help of hotshot lawyer Mike, suddenly it's not just her future at stake—it's her heart....

### #4360 A BRIDE FOR THE MAVERICK MILLIONAIRE
*Journey Through the Outback*
**Marion Lennox**
From relaxing cruise to thrilling Outback adventure, Finn takes Rachel on a wild ride! But Rachel's still reeling from her painful past....

### #4361 SHIPWRECKED WITH MR. WRONG
**Nikki Logan**
Rob and Honor couldn't be more opposite! But marooned in paradise, Honor discovers that even playboys have their good points....

### #4362 WHEN CHOCOLATE IS NOT ENOUGH...
**Nina Harrington**
For Daisy and Flynn their chocolate business deal equals their ultimate dream. But soon they're tempted by something even sweeter....

You can find more information on upcoming Harlequin®
titles, free excerpts and more at www.Harlequin.com.          HRCNM1212

# REQUEST YOUR FREE BOOKS!
## 2 FREE NOVELS PLUS 2 FREE GIFTS!

**Harlequin®**

*Romance*

### From the Heart, For the Heart

**YES!** Please send me 2 FREE Harlequin® Romance novels and my 2 FREE gifts (gifts are worth about $10). After receiving them, if I don't wish to receive any more books, I can return the shipping statement marked "cancel". If I don't cancel, I will receive 6 brand-new novels every month and be billed just $4.09 per book in the U.S. or $4.49 per book in Canada. That's a savings of at least 14% off the cover price! It's quite a bargain! Shipping and handling is just 50¢ per book in the U.S. and 75¢ per book in Canada.* I understand that accepting the 2 free books and gifts places me under no obligation to buy anything. I can always return a shipment and cancel at any time. Even if I never buy another book, the two free books and gifts are mine to keep forever.

116/316 HDN FESE

| | |
|---|---|
| Name | (PLEASE PRINT) |

| | | |
|---|---|---|
| Address | | Apt. # |

| | | |
|---|---|---|
| City | State/Prov. | Zip/Postal Code |

Signature (if under 18, a parent or guardian must sign)

### Mail to the **Reader Service**:
**IN U.S.A.:** P.O. Box 1867, Buffalo, NY 14240-1867
**IN CANADA:** P.O. Box 609, Fort Erie, Ontario L2A 5X3

Not valid for current subscribers to Harlequin Romance books.

**Are you a subscriber to Harlequin Romance books
and want to receive the larger-print edition?
Call 1-800-873-8635 or visit www.ReaderService.com.**

* Terms and prices subject to change without notice. Prices do not include applicable taxes. Sales tax applicable in N.Y. Canadian residents will be charged applicable taxes. Offer not valid in Quebec. This offer is limited to one order per household. All orders subject to credit approval. Credit or debit balances in a customer's account(s) may be offset by any other outstanding balance owed by or to the customer. Please allow 4 to 6 weeks for delivery. Offer available while quantities last.

**Your Privacy**—The Reader Service is committed to protecting your privacy. Our Privacy Policy is available online at www.ReaderService.com or upon request from the Reader Service.

We make a portion of our mailing list available to reputable third parties that offer products we believe may interest you. If you prefer that we not exchange your name with third parties, or if you wish to clarify or modify your communication preferences, please visit us at www.ReaderService.com/consumerschoice or write to us at Reader Service Preference Service, P.O. Box 9062, Buffalo, NY 14269. Include your complete name and address.

HRIIB

*One unbreakable legacy divides two powerful kingdoms....*

*Read on for a sneak peek at*
*BEHOLDEN TO THE THRONE by* USA TODAY
*bestselling author Carol Marinelli.*

\* \* \*

"Let's go now to the tent and make love...." Emir's mind stilled when he tasted her lips; the pleasure he had forgone he now remembered. Except this was different, for he tasted not a woman, but Amy. He liked the still of her breath as his mouth shocked her, liked the fight for control beneath his hands, for her mouth was still but her body was succumbing. He felt her pause momentarily, and then she gave in to him. But there was something unexpected, an emotion he had never tasted in a woman before—all the anger she had held in check was delivered to him in her response. A savage kiss met him now, a different kiss than one he was used to. The gentle lovemaking he had intended, the tender seduction he had pictured, changed as she kissed him back.

"Please..." The word spilled from her lips. It sounded like begging. "Take me back...."

Except he wanted her now. His hands were at the buttons of her robe, pulling it down over her shoulders, their kisses frantic, their want building.

She grappled with his robe, felt the leather that held his sword and the power of the man who was about to make love to her. She was kissing a king and it terrified her, but still it was delicious, still it inflamed as his words attempted to soothe.

"The people will come to accept…" he said, kissing her neck, moving down to her exposed skin so that she ached for his mouth to soothe there, ached to give in to his mastery, but her mind struggled to fathom his words.

"The people…?"

"When I take you as my bride."

"Bride!" He might as well have pushed her into the water. She felt the plunge into confusion and struggled to come up for air, felt the horror as history repeated—for it was happening again.

"Emir, no…"

"Yes." He must know she was overwhelmed by his offer, but he didn't seem to recognize that she was dying in his arms as his mouth moved back to take her again, to calm her. But as she spoke he froze.

"I can't have children…."

\* \* \*

*Can Amy stop at one night only with the enigmatic emir?
Especially when this ruler drives a hard bargain—
one that's nonnegotiable…?*

*Pick up
BEHOLDEN TO THE THRONE
by Carol Marinelli on December 18, 2012,
from Harlequin® Presents®.*

HPEXP1212

# RAYE MORGAN

*brings you a touching story*
*of trust and new love.*

Marc Huntington needs to protect his
ancestral home when he discovers it's being
sold. Luckily, keeping an eye on the main
competition is no hardship: Torie Sands
is as beautiful as she is secretive....

Torie's back to clear her family's name—
not to fall for Marc! How will she gain the trust
of this hard, suspicious man, whose years as a
navy SEAL have left him wounded and wary?

## THE HEIR'S PROPOSAL
*Available January 2, 2013.*